LOVE, LORDS,
AND
LADY-BIRDS

Dutton Books by Barbara Cartland

Love Locked In
The Wild, Unwilling Wife
The Passion and the Flower
Love, Lords, and Lady-Birds

Barbara Cartland

LOVE, LORDS, AND AND LADY-BIRDS

E. P. DUTTON
New York

Library of Congress Cataloging in Publication Data

Cartland, Barbara, 1902-
    Love, lords, and lady-birds.

    I. Title.
PZ3.C247Lt3   [PR6005.A765]   823'.9'12   77-7027

ISBN: 0-525-14920-1

Published simultaneously in Canada by Clarke, Irwin & Company Limited, Toronto and Vancouver

10 9 8 7 6 5 4 3 2 1

First Edition

Author's Note

A book called *A People's Conscience* by Strathearn
Gordon and T. G. B. Cock describes six typical en-
quiries during 1729–1837 by Select Committees of the
House of Commons, from which I have taken the
references in this novel. Little or nothing was done for
the plight of the child prostitutes and in Victorian times
their condition was worse than ever.

Paradise Row, with its centuries-old history of famous residents, was demolished in 1906. Vauxhall
Gardens ceased to be an attraction in 1859. It was
closed, and the grounds, which had seen so many spec-
tacular entertainments and so many distinguished
guests, was built on. The references to the Fire Police
and the Fire Brigades of the period are all accurate,
as are the descriptions of the newspapers of that year.

LOVE, LORDS,
AND
LADY-BIRDS

Chapter One
1819

The off-side leader went lame and the Earl of Staverton swore beneath his breath. Then he pulled his horses to a standstill and his groom jumped down from the seat behind the Phaeton.

"It'll likely be a stone, M'Lord," he said cheerfully as he ran forward. "These roads be terrible bad."

"Bad indeed!" the Earl replied, repressing more-forceful language.

He tied the reins to the front of the Phaeton and stepped down.

The road was in fact extremely stony and he was not surprised that one of the stones had lodged in the horse's hoof.

He thought perhaps he had been driving imprudently fast over such a rough surface, but he was in a hurry to get to London and away from the boredom he had endured in the house where he had been staying near St. Albans for a mill between two well-known pugilists.

It had been an excellent fight and the Earl had backed the winner for a considerable sum of money.

But both the company of his host and the food provided had been one long yawn from start to finish.

Admittedly the Earl was not easily amused, and he found a great many things and a large number of people to be what he termed a "dead bore."

It was a pleasant spring morning. Wild flowers were to be seen in plenty amongst the grasses at the side of the road, and there were primroses in the hedgerows and bluebells making an azure carpet under the trees in the wood.

The Earl watched as his groom prised out the sharp stone which had lodged in the hoof carefully so as not to loosen the shoe.

He looked at his team with pleasure. Jet black and perfectly matched, they were, he knew, the most outstanding horse-flesh to be seen in the Four-In-Hand Club, which he was confident no other member was able to match.

To stretch his legs he walked through the grasses, regardless of the fact that the pollen marked his shining Hessians, which had been polished with champagne as originally decreed by Beau Brummell.

On one side of him there was a brick wall, higher than was usual, enclosing the Park of some important aristocrat.

The bricks, narrow and originally red, had mellowed with time and the wall was now deep pink in colour, which told the Earl, who was an expert on antiques, that it was Elizabethan.

The spring sunlight playing on the bricks was in fact very beautiful, and he was just wishing that the wall that enclosed Staverton House in Oxfordshire was the same colour when suddenly a heavy object flew past his head, missing by inches.

It fell with a thud at his feet and he looked down with astonishment to see that it was a leather valise not too heavy to carry, but doubtless a dangerous weapon should it have struck him.

He looked to where it had come from and saw climbing over the top of the wall a female figure.

There was a most improper expanse of very shapely legs before the owner dropped to the ground with a lithe grace which kept her on her feet and prevented her from sprawling, as might have been expected, on her back.

She had descended with her face to the wall and only as she turned round did she see the Earl with the valise at his feet.

"That was an extremely dangerous thing to do," he said coldly. "If it had hit me I could easily have been knocked out."

"How was I to know that anyone would be standing near the only place where it is possible to climb the wall?" she asked.

She walked towards him as she spoke and he saw that she carried her bonnet on her arm and her hair was gold with red lights in it.

As she looked up at him, her eyes were very large and there was something mischievous in the way they slanted a little at the corners. Her mouth also curved, which gave her an unmistakably impish expression.

She was not strictly beautiful, but she had, he thought, a decidedly fascinating face, quite different from that of any girl he had seen before.

"I presume that you are running away," the Earl remarked.

"I should hardly be likely to climb the wall if I could walk out through the gate!" was the reply.

She bent down, intending to retrieve her valise, and at that moment saw the Earl's horses.

"Are those yours?" she asked in an awe-struck tone.

"They are," he answered, "but the leader has collected a stone, owing to your abominable roads."

"Not mine!" the girl retorted. "But they are wonderful! The most magnificent horses I have ever seen!"

"I am honoured that you should think so," the Earl said with a sarcastic twist to his lips.

"Where are you going?"

"To London, as it happens."

"Then please ... please take me with you. That is where I wish to go, and I would like above all else to drive behind such an exceptional team."

She moved towards them as she spoke, forgetting the valise, which still lay on the grass at the Earl's feet.

"I feel it is my duty to ask you from whom you are running away and why," the Earl said.

The girl had drawn nearer to the horses and was standing looking at them, her eyes shining.

"They are superb!" she breathed. "How can you have found four such perfect matches?"

"I asked you a question," the Earl persisted.

"What about?" she enquired absent-mindedly, then added:

"I am running away from School, and unless they are to find out that I have gone, we should be moving."

"I do not wish to become involved in anything reprehensible," the Earl said.

"That sounds very stuffy," she replied scornfully, "but if you will not take me, then Jeb the butcher will. He should be along at any time now."

"You have an assignation with him?"

"No, but I have talked to him about his horses and I know he will oblige me."

She looked down the road as she spoke, then her eyes came back to the Earl's face.

"Please take me," she begged. "Nothing you can say or do will make me go back, so it is either you or Jeb. But I would like so much to drive with you."

As she spoke, the Earl's groom straightened his back.

"It'll be all right now, M'Lord."

The girl's eyes were still on the Earl's face.

"Please," she pleaded almost beneath her breath.

"I will take you on one condition," the Earl said.

"What is that?"

"That you tell me why you are running away, and if I do not consider it a really valid excuse I shall take you back."

"You could not be so treacherous!" she exclaimed.

"At the same time, my reason is a really good one."

"It had better be," the Earl said grimly.

He helped her into the Phaeton and undid the reins.

The groom picked up the valise, stowed it away at the back as he swung himself into the high, chair-like seat that he himself occupied, and they were off.

They drove a little way in silence and the Earl was aware that his companion was not thinking of him but of his horses.

"I am waiting," he remarked.

"For what?"

"You know quite well what for, and I have a feeling you are deliberately prolonging your explanation so as to be carried as far away from your School as possible before you tell me."

She flashed him a smile which made her lips curve most beguilingly.

"That is quite intelligent of you!"

"I am not as obtuse as you appear to think," the Earl answered sarcastically. "Who are you meeting when you reach London?"

His companion gave a little laugh.

"I wish I could tell you it was some ardent Beau, but I can assure you that if there were one I would have made him fetch me from School and not have to rely on Jeb or the lucky chance of meeting a stranger like yourself."

"No Beau? Then why this anxiety to get to London?"

"Because I am too old to be at School any longer, and my horrible, beastly Guardian insists that I spend all my holidays in Harrogate."

"What is wrong with Harrogate?" the Earl asked.

"Everything is wrong with Harrogate! It is dull, it is full of very old and ill people. When I was there for the Christmas holidays, I never met a single man except for the Vicar!"

Her tone was so scathing that the Earl laughed despite himself.

"You have obviously suffered acutely in such a place," he said, "but is there nowhere else you could go?"

"Not as far as my Guardian is concerned," the girl answered. "The loathsome creature does not even answer my letters, and every suggestion I make is rejected by his Lawyer."

"He sounds somewhat unfeeling," the Earl agreed. "When you reach London are you intending to beard him in person?"

"Certainly not! I have no intention of going near him, and I suspect that the reason why he does not want to see me or communicate with me is that he is spending my fortune on himself."

The Earl turned to look at her speculatively. As he took in the plain bonnet with its dark blue ribbons and the simple, unimaginative gown, the girl said passionately:

"You are thinking I do not look like an heiress, and is it surprising when my clothes are chosen for me by Cousin Adelaide, who is nearly eighty, and paid for by my Guardian's Lawyer?"

Her lips tightened before she went on:

"I was eighteen last week and all my friends—my real friends—made their débuts last year. I was still in mourning for Papa so I suppose there was some excuse for not allowing me to be presented at Court then, but this year I was sure that I would be allowed to go to London."

"What are your Guardian's reasons for refusing?"

"I told you, I never hear from the brute! I wrote him pages and pages after Christmas and his Lawyer simply replied that I was to stay at School until further notice."

She drew in her breath, then continued:

"I waited until now—three months—and now I have made an important decision. I will take the matter into my own hands."

"And when you reach London what do you intend to do?" the Earl asked.

"I am going to become a Lady-Bird!"

"A—Lady-Bird?" he questioned.

"That is what Claire's brother Rupert calls them, but I believe another description is 'a bit o' muslin' or a 'Cyprian.' "

The Earl was so astonished that for a moment he let the reins fall loose and his horses broke into a gallop.

He steadied them again before he asked:

"Have you the least idea of what you are saying?"

"Of course I have!" his companion replied. "As I am not allowed to take my place in Society, I shall make my life in my own way."

"I cannot believe you know what you are implying."

"My best friend Claire explained it all to me last year before she left," his companion replied. "All the smart Beaux have mistresses and that means the lady they choose is expected to belong to them and to no-one else. A Lady-Bird can pick and choose. If one man bores her she can find another one who is more interesting."

"And you really believe that sort of—life would suit you?" the Earl asked, choosing his words with care.

"It must be more amusing than sitting in that deadly School, having already learnt everything they can possibly teach me. Of course I shall be very careful in selecting the man with whom I shall spend my time."

"I should hope so!" the Earl remarked.

"Think what fun it will be to do what I like, and not permanently have people telling me that everything I want to do is wrong and unconventional."

"What do you imagine you will do?"

"Go to Vauxhall, for one thing, and see the fireworks. Drive my own Phaeton in the Park, dance every night, have a house of my own, and not have to worry as to whether I get married or not."

"You have no wish to be married?"

"Of course not! It would be worse than being a mistress to be tied up with one man forever! Claire says that Society is nothing more than a marriage-market anyway."

"What does your friend Claire mean by that?"

"She says that every débutante is competing either to marry a nit-wit because he has a title or some fat, red-faced old man because he is rich. That at least is one thing I do not have to worry about. I have a huge fortune all my own."

"Surely, if that is the truth, your Guardian will allow you to spend some of it?"

"I told you, he does not answer my letters. His Lawyer tells me to send him my bills and they are then paid. But what I want is cash in my hand."

"I should have thought there might be better ways of obtaining it than taking up the profession of which you speak."

"Profession?" the girl queried. "Is being a Lady-Bird a profession, like being a Doctor or a Lawyer? How interesting!"

The Earl thought of quite a number of retorts he might have made to a more sophisticated woman, but instead he went on driving with a frown between his eyes.

He was wondering what he could say to this impulsive child who, he was certain, had not the least idea of the implications of what she was intending.

He could imagine the perils she might have encountered had she found herself in the company of the more raffish and at times dissolute young men who drove about the countryside from Race-Meeting to Race-Meeting, merely to see what excitements they could find.

"You have not told me your name," he said after a moment.

"Petrina . . ." she replied, and stopped.

"You must have another name."

"As I have told you so much about myself, I think it would be unwise to let you know any more. After all, you might have been a friend of my father's."

"In which case I should undoubtedly try to dissuade you from this disgraceful idea."

"Nothing is going to stop me now," Petrina answered. "I have made up my mind, and when I have established myself I might get in touch with my Guardian."

"I imagine you will have to if you want some money."

Petrina gave a little chuckle.

"I wondered if you would think of that. I thought of it myself, and that is why I waited so long before setting out for London."

"What have you done?"

"I have collected quite a considerable sum through sheer cleverness."

"How?"

"I sent bills to the Lawyers which I had made up myself."

"What sort of bills?"

"Bills for books, for School uniforms, for all sorts of

miscellaneous things. I thought they might be suspicious, but they paid up quite happily."

There was so much triumph in the young voice that the Earl could not help smiling.

"I can see you are extremely resourceful, Petrina."

"I have to be," she answered. "Now that my Papa and Mama are dead, I have no relatives left except poor old Cousin Adelaide, who really has one foot in the grave."

The Earl did not reply, and after a moment she went on:

"I am sure I have enough money to get myself settled. Then, when I am the Talk of the Town, there will be nothing my Guardian can do but hand over my fortune.'"

"Supposing he refuses?"

Petrina gave a little sigh.

"Of course, he might do that, in which case I shall have to wait until I am twenty-one, when I get half of it, or twenty-five, when I get the whole."

"I have a feeling that, as in most wills, there is a proviso if you marry."

"Of course," Petrina agreed, "and that is why I have no intention of getting married and handing all my money over to a husband to do what he likes with it."

She paused before she added scornfully:

"He might be like my Guardian and keep it all to himself, giving me nothing."

"All men are not like that," the Earl remarked mildly.

"Claire says that Society is full of money-grubbers, young aristocrats who are on the look-out for a rich wife to keep them. I shall fare far better as a Lady-Bird . . . I am quite certain of that."

"As you seem to have a very low opinion of the male sex," the Earl remarked, "I cannot imagine that you will find the men with whom you associate particularly attractive."

Petrina thought this over for a moment, then she said:

"I need not make big financial demands upon them. Claire's brother told her that his mistress costs him a fortune every year. She demands carriages, horses, a house in Chelsea, and masses of jewellery, far more than he can afford."

"I do not know who Claire's brother may be," the Earl said, "but I should not take his description of the *Beau Monde* as entirely reliable."

"He is Viscount Coombe," Petrina said, "and Claire says he is a very Tulip of Fashion."

That was one of the few accurate things Petrina had said so far, the Earl thought.

He knew the Viscount and thought him a pleasant but rather stupid young man, who was wasting his allowance from his father, the Marquess of Morecombe, in a spend-thrift manner which had not gone unnoticed in the Clubs of St. James's.

As if she knew by his silence what he was thinking, Petrina said:

"You know Rupert!"

"I have met him," the Earl admitted.

"Claire thought he would do me very well as a husband, especially as he is always wanting money. But as I explained to her, I do not want a husband, I want to be independent."

"I think you must realise that that is utterly impossible," the Earl said.

"How do other women become Lady-Birds?"

"They are not usually heiresses to start with."

"It is no use being an heiress if you cannot get your fingers on your own money," Petrina said with inescapable logic.

"If you take my advice," the Earl said, "I suggest

that before you do anything drastic you call and see your Guardian."

"What shall I gain by that?" Petrina asked. "He will doubtless be so annoyed by my leaving School that he will send me back under armed guard. Then I shall have to escape all over again."

"I think if you explain to him that you are too old to be at School any longer and that all your friends have made their débuts, he will see reason."

"Reason!" Petrina snorted. "He has not seen reason up until now. Why, why out of all the men in the whole world, should Papa have chosen him to be my Guardian? I expect he is old, strait-laced, and doubtless religious as well, so he will disapprove of anything amusing."

"Why should you think he will be like that?"

"Because Papa, having lived an exciting and adventurous life himself, wanted to protect me. He was always saying: 'When you grow up, my darling, you must never make the mistakes I have.' "

"And had he made a lot of mistakes?"

"I do not think so. Not as far as I was concerned," Petrina answered. "But he fought quite a number of duels over beautiful ladies and I expect he was referring to them."

She gave a little exclamation and flung out her hands.

"Whatever it was, here am I saddled with this beastly old Guardian! When I think of all my money locked up in his safe or hidden under his bed, I could scream!"

They drove on for a little while in silence. Then the Earl said:

"I told you I have no desire to become involved in your mad escapade, and I make no promises, but perhaps, seeing the circumstances in which we have met, I could speak to your Guardian."

Petrina turned round to stare at him in surprise, her eyes very wide.

"Would you really do that?" she asked. "That is kind of you! I take back all the things I have been thinking about you!"

"What were you thinking?" the Earl asked curiously.

"I thought you were rather top-lofty, stiff-necked, the grand old man stuffed with wisdom, condescending to the poor little peasant girl who knows no better."

The Earl laughed as if he could not help himself.

"You are the most incorrigible brat I have ever met in my life! I cannot believe that you are really serious in your intensions; and yet, because you are so obviously unpredictable, I am half-afraid that you are serious."

"I am entirely serious," Petrina assured him. "And if you go to see my Guardian I shall hide myself, so that if he says no, he will not be able to find me and I can go on with my own plans."

"Your own plans are not only entirely impractical, they are exceedingly reprehensible," the Earl said sharply, "and would not be considered by any woman who calls herself a lady."

Petrina laughed.

"I knew we would get round sooner or later to the subject of being a lady. 'A lady does not go out walking without her gloves.' 'A lady never answers back.' 'A lady does not walk in the street unescorted or go dancing until she is fully grown-up!' I am fed up with hearing about ladies! They lead the most boring, dull, restricted lives. I want to be free!"

"The sort of freedom which you envisage for yourself is absolutely impossible."

"Only because you think I am a lady."

"Well, you are, and there is nothing you can do about it."

"Except behave like a Lady-Bird."

She was silent for a moment, then she said speculatively:

"I cannot help wondering how they do behave, but I expect I shall see lots of them in London. Claire says I shall recognise them because they are usually very smart, very pretty, and drive in the Park unattended."

She paused and glanced at the Earl from under her eye-lashes as she added:

"Except by gentlemen, of course."

"But the women to whom you are referring are not ladies, and they certainly do not have fortunes like yours to fall back on."

"Think how pleased the gentlemen will be if they do not have to provide me with carriages and lots and lots of jewellery!"

The Earl did not answer and after a moment she asked:

"How much does your mistress cost you a year?"

Once again the Earl was startled into almost losing control of his horses, then he said sharply:

"You are not to ask such questions! You are not to talk· about such women! You are to behave yourself! Do you understand?"

"Because you say so?" Petrina asked. "You have no jurisdiction over me, as you well know."

"I can refuse to take you any farther," the Earl threatened.

Petrina looked round her with a smile.

They had joined the main highway to London and there was quite a considerable amount of traffic not only of private Phaetons and carriages, but post-chaises and stage-coaches.

"If I had any sense," the Earl averred, "I would put you down and leave you to go to the devil your own way."

Petrina laughed.

"I am not afraid, if that is what you want to do. Now that I am so near to London, I can take a stage-coach or hire a post-chaise to go the rest of the way."

"And when you reach London, where do you intend to stay?"

"At a Hotel."

"No respectable Hotel would have you."

"I know the name of one that will," Petrina retorted. "Rupert told Claire it was where he had sometimes stayed with a Lady-Bird, so I do not think they will refuse me."

The trouble with the Viscount Coombe, the Earl thought angrily, was that he talked far too freely in front of his sister.

"Have you heard of the Griffin Hotel off Jermyn Street?" Petrina asked.

The Earl had, and he knew it was not the sort of environment for a young woman alone, least of all anyone as young and unsophisticated as Petrina.

"I am going to take you straight to your Guardian," he said aloud. "I will explain your predicament to him, and I think I can promise that at least he will listen to me, and I hope will behave in a reasonable manner."

"He might, if you are of sufficient importance," Petrina said after a moment, "and I think you must be to have horses like yours."

"What is your Guardian's name?" the Earl asked.

Petrina did not answer for a moment and he knew she was considering whether she could trust him or not.

Because of her reluctance, he felt himself begin to lost control of his temper.

"Dammit all! I am doing my best to help you," he said. "Any other girl would be grateful to me."

"I am grateful to you for bringing me as far as this," Petrina answered slowly.

"Then why are you so reluctant to trust me?"

"It is not that, it is just because I think that you are so old you have forgotten how to be young."

The Earl squared his chin.

'Old!' he thought. 'Old at thirty-three!' But he supposed that was what a child of eighteen would think. At the same time, it was a sobering thought.

Then he looked at Petrina and saw the mischief in her eyes.

"You are deliberately provoking me!" he said accusingly.

"Well, you have been so supercilious and stuck-up the whole way here," she complained, "talking down to me as if I had not a brain in my head. I may tell you I am considered to be extremely intelligent."

"What you are contemplating is not in the least intelligent," he snapped.

"I think I have got under your skin," she teased, "and it delights me."

"Why?"

"I suppose because you are so omnipotent—so immune to the troubles and difficulties of ordinary human beings like me. You make me want to throw stones at you."

"Then it is a pity you missed me with your valise," the Earl replied. "I might have lain unconscious on the ground while you found yourself under arrest for assault."

Petrina smiled at him mockingly.

"I should not have waited to be arrested. I should have run away."

"Something you seem to be particularly good at!"

"Well, I have not done badly for a first attempt, have I? Here I am, driving to London behind the most magnificent horses I have ever seen, with . . ."

She stopped speaking and turned to look at him.

She took in for the first time the snowy-white, intricately tied cravat with the points of his collar high against his chin-bone, the superb grey whip-cord driving-coat, the tightly fitting yellow pantaloons, and the high-crowned hat set at an angle on his dark head.

"I know what you are," she cried. "You are a Corinthian! I always hoped I should meet one."

"Instead of talking about me," the Earl said, "I am waiting for you first to tell me the name of your Guardian, then your own name."

"Very well, I will risk it," Petrina answered, "and if the worst comes to the worst I can always run away so that you cannot find me."

"That will be difficult for you if you become the Talk of the Town, as you intend."

She chuckled again.

"You are rather good at repartee. I like it when you snap back."

As the Earl was noted for having a very ready wit and his *bons mots* were invariably repeated round the Clubs after he had made them, this artless remark made his lips curve cynically, but he said nothing, only waited.

"Very well," Petrina sighed. "The name of my horrible, cruel, beastly Guardian is the Earl of Staverton!"

"I might have expected it!" the Earl thought.

It was as if everything that had happened had built up to this moment.

Slowly, almost as if the words were forced from his lips, he said:

"Then your name is Lyndon—and your father was Lucky Lyndon!"

"How did you know that?"

Petrina's eyes were wide.

"Because it is I who have the misfortune to be your Guardian!"

"I do not believe it! It is not possible! You are not old enough, for one thing."

"A moment ago you were telling me I was too old!"

"But I thought you would be decrepit, have white hair, and walk with a stick."

"I am sorry if I disappoint you."

"Then if you are really my Guardian, what have you done with my money?"

"I assure you that it is, to the best of my knowledge, intact," the Earl said.

"Then why . . . why have you behaved in such a horrible manner to me?"

"To tell the truth, I had actually forgotten your existence," the Earl replied.

He felt Petrina stiffen as if at the insult and went on to explain:

"As it happened, I was abroad when your father died, and when I returned I had a great many personal matters to attend to because I had only just inherited my father's title and estates. I am afraid your problems were set aside for mine."

"But you must have told your Lawyer that I was to go to Harrogate in the holidays and stay with Cousin Adelaide."

"I told him to deal with the matter as he thought best."

"But you knew Papa?"

"Your father and I served in the same Regiment, and before the Battle of Waterloo a great number of us made wills. Those who were married left their children, and sometimes even their wives, in the charge of friends whom they thought most capable of looking after them if they were killed."

"Papa was older than you."

"Quite a deal older," the Earl agreed, "but we played cards together and we both had a great love of horses."

"And because you knew a lot about horse-flesh, Papa thought you were a suitable Guardian for me," Petrina said bitterly. "Well, I only hope he is aware, in Heaven or wherever he is, what a mess you have made of it."

"I am astonished that your father never changed his will."

"I suppose he thought there was no-one else more suitable. Anyway, he did not expect to die when he did."

"No, of course not. Was it an accident?"

"He had been drinking with friends and when they rode home someone bet Papa he would not jump a very high wall. Papa never could resist a bet."

"I am sorry."

"I loved him," Petrina said, "although he was often very unpredictable."

"And your mother?"

"She died during the war when Papa was with Wellington's Army."

"And that left only Cousin Adelaide."

"Yes, Cousin Adelaide," Petrina agreed in a different tone of voice, "and no-one except you could think her a suitable companion for a young girl."

"I suppose I shall have to allow you to choose your own Chaperon," the Earl said.

"I am not going to have one!"

"Oh yes you are!" he replied. "As your Guardian I shall appoint one immediately, and if you are pleasant to me I will allow you to have a choice in the matter."

Petrina looked at him suspiciously.

"Are you intending to launch me on Society?"

"I suppose I shall have to," he replied, "but let me assure you, Petrina, I have no desire to do so! I cannot imagine what I shall do, saddled with a débutante, especially one like you."

"I do not want to be a débutante, I want to be a Lady-Bird."

"If I hear one more mention of that," the Earl

said firmly, "I shall give you a good spanking, which, incidentally, is something which I imagine has been regrettably omitted from your education in the past."

"If you are going to take that attitude towards me," Petrina retorted, "I shall run away here and now, and you will never find me again."

"Then I shall hang on to your fortune," the Earl said. "You have already accused me of spending it on myself."

"Have you done so?"

"No, of course not! I happen to be an extremely wealthy man."

"Then I would like everything I own handed over to me immediately."

"You get half, I think, when you are twenty-one, and the rest when you are twenty-five, or the whole lot when you marry."

Petrina stamped her foot on the floor of the Phaeton.

"You are only quoting to me my own words. I wish I had known who you were when I was waiting for Jeb."

"Think how lucky you have been," the Earl said mockingly. "By sheer coincidence I have turned out, as if we were in a fairy-story, to be your Guardian. I have waved my magic wand, you come to London, make your curtsey to the Queen at Buckingham Palace, and, if you wish, to the Regent. You are then launched into the *Beau Monde.*"

"You mean everyone will pay a great deal of attention to me because I am your Ward?"

"And you are also, of course, an heiress," the Earl said.

"I am not going to marry anyone, even if you do plan to find me a suitable husband."

"If you imagine I am going to concern myself with your amatory adventures, you are very much mistaken!" the Earl retorted. "I will find you a Chaperon,

and as my house is very large I presume you can live
there for the time being. If you annoy me or are tiresome, I shall rent a house for you on your own."

"Shall I never see you?" Petrina asked curiously.

"Not often," the Earl answered frankly. "I have
a well-organised life, a great deal to do one way or
another, and frankly I find young girls a bore!"

"If they are anything like the girls I was at School
with, I am not surprised," Petrina said. "But I suppose they grow up into the witty, sophisticated women
of the world with whom you have tempestuous love-
affairs."

"Who told you that?" the Earl asked in a voice of
thunder.

"Claire said that all the Gentlemen of Fashion had
mistresses—after all, what about the Regent? And
all the most beautiful women have lovers."

"If you would cease quoting your foolish and
ill-informed friend I think we would get along a great
deal better," the Earl said irritably.

"But it is true, is it not?" Petrina enquired.

"What is true?"

"That you have made love to lots and lots of beautiful ladies."

This was undeniably a fact, but it made the Earl
extremely annoyed.

"Will you stop talking about things no well-behaved
girl should mention?" he stormed. "When I launch
you in Society, Petrina, you will be ostracised by all
the most important hostesses if you speak of mistresses and all the other vulgar creatures you have
mentioned since we met each other."

"I think you are very unfair," Petrina complained.
"After all, you kept asking me questions and I answered truthfully. It is no use complaining now that
I did not lie. How was I to know you were my
guardian?"

With an effort the Earl controlled his temper.

"I cannot believe that any girl with your opportunities would not wish to be a success, and it will be impossible to be one unless you learn to cure your tongue."

"I have had to curb it at School," Petrina replied, "but I had hoped when I got away I should be able to be myself, and I do not see really why that is wrong."

"Your whole attitude is wrong," the Earl said severely. "Nicely behaved, well-brought-up young ladies make their début and get married, and know nothing about the seamy side of life."

"You mean about Lady-Birds, and 'bits o' muslin'?"

"Yes!"

"Well, Claire knows all about them."

"Claire has a brother who obviously has a very irresponsible attitude towards his sister."

"I have a feeling Rupert and I would have a great deal in common."

"Perhaps you will," the Earl replied. "In which case he might wish to marry you, and as he will be the Marquess of Morecombe one day, I should give such an alliance my whole-hearted consent."

"There you go!" Petrina exclaimed. "Talking just like some cackling old Dowager who is thrusting her daughter upon the marriage-market!"

She made a sound of contempt and went on:

"Rupert wants my money, and you think I want his title. Well, let me make it quite clear, my dear Guardian, I have no intention of marrying anyone unless I come to feel very different from what I feel about men at the moment."

"Of whom you know nothing, except for a Vicar."

"There you go again, quoting my own words at me! All right . . . of whom I know nothing. But even in

London they must have heard of something called Love."

"I am surprised you have heard of it. It is the first time you have mentioned that elusive emotion."

"I have thought about it," Petrina said seriously. "I have thought about it quite a lot."

"I am very glad to hear it."

"But I feel it may be something which I shall never experience."

"Why?" the Earl asked.

"Because when the girls at School talked about love they were all so sloppy. They would talk about some man they had met in the holidays as if he were an Adonis. They used to go to bed with his name written on a piece of paper under their pillow, and hope they would dream of him. Claire was even kissed!"

"I might have guessed that," the Earl said sarcastically.

"She said the first time it happened was very disappointing, not a bit what she had expected. The second was better, but not really romantic."

"What did she expect?" the Earl asked furiously.

"Something like Dante felt for Beatrice, or Romeo for Juliet, but I have a feeling ordinary men are not like that.'"

There was silence. Then Petrina said:

"I have decided that no-one shall kiss me until I really want them to. Of course I should like them to try, then I shall have the satisfaction of turning them down."

"The truth is that your outlook on life is one of complete ignorance," the Earl said scathingly. "You only know what your friend Claire has told you, most of which she has learnt second-hand from her brother. My advice is for you to start again without a lot of preconceived poppycock ideas."

"Of course, things may be better than I anticipate."

"I certainly hope they will be."

"May I have lots of new gowns?"

"As many as you like, since you will be paying for them."

She gave a little sigh of satisfaction.

"I shall enjoy having men look at me with admiration, and of course laughing at what I say because I am so witty."

"I have not been very impressed by anything you have said so far," the Earl commented.

"I have not had much opportunity yet, but once I get into the swing of things I expect it will come naturally."

"I hope not," the Earl replied. "What you say naturally makes me shudder."

"You take things far too seriously," Petrina said. "As I have already said, you have forgotten how to be young and carefree. If I am really going to make my début, as you suggest, I am determined to be the most outstanding, the most exciting, and certainly the most talked-about débutante London has ever known!"

"That is just what I am afraid of!" the Earl said with a groan.

"Now you are being stiff-necked and top-lofty again," Petrina said derisively.

Chapter Two

When they arrived in London and drove down Park
Lane, Petrina was watching everything with sparkling
eyes.

She had been in London several times in her life,
but her father's house was in Worcestershire and she
had forgotten how crowded the streets were and how
colourful everything appeared.

When she saw Staverton House she stared at it in
astonishment.

Never had she thought that anyone she knew would
live in so impressive a mansion.

It stood on the corner of Upper Grosvenor Street
and Park Lane and occupied three acres.

The entrance had a majestic stone screen com-
posed of eight columns with lamp-posts in between
each of them.

There was a carriage entrance protected by superb
metal gates surmounted by pediments bearing the family crest.

"Do you live here all alone?" Petrina asked, looking at the West and East wings of the house ranging
out from the centre block.

There was a note of awe in her voice which made
the Earl reply:

"I am glad something about me has impressed you."

When she entered the huge marble Hall and saw the doors of solid mahogany picked out in gold, the mantelpieces of Carrara marble, and the tables of lapis lazuli mounted on ormolu, Petrina was even more impressed.

She was to learn later that the house contained the finest collection of Rembrandts in the country, besides paintings by Velazquez and Rubens.

In the Salon there were Italian, French, Dutch, and Flemish pictures, and in the Small Drawing-Room hung two of Gainsborough's masterpieces and Sir Joshua Reynolds's portrait of Mrs. Siddons.

But this Petrina did not know at the moment; she only felt awed and somehow insignificant, which made her put up her chin defiantly.

"Welcome home, M'Lord!" A Major Domo bowed, resplendent in gold braid on the black and gold livery which was worn by an inordinate number of flunkeys, all over six foot tall.

"Send Mr. Richardson to me immediately!" the Earl commanded as he took off his hat and gloves.

"I should inform Your Lordship that Her Grace the Duchess of Kingston arrived this afternoon," the Major Domo said in respectful tones.

"What could be more opportune?" the Earl exclaimed, and added to Petrina:

"My grandmother is here, which we might say is an extremely fortunate coincidence."

"Her Grace is resting," the Major Domo interposed.

"Tell Mrs. Meadows to look after Miss Lyndon," the Earl ordered, and walked up the curving staircase, passing a fine collection of portraits which had been commissioned by his father from contemporary artists.

On reaching the landing he turned towards the West

Wing, where his guests were always accommodated so as to be as far away as possible from his own private part of the house.

Here two rooms were kept exclusively for his grandmother's use whenever she wished to visit London.

She was, the Earl found, seated comfortably in an arm-chair in the attractive Sitting-Room which adjoined her bed-room. It was fragrant with the scent of hot-house flowers sent to London from the greenhouses on the Earl's country estate.

As if she had been expecting him, the Dowager Duchess looked up as her grandson entered, and there was no mistaking the smile of welcome on her face.

The Dowager Duchess had been a great beauty.

The Duke of Kingston had fallen in love with her on sight and married her at midnight at the Mayfair Chapel so that there could be no opposition or protests from his family, who had expected him to make a far more advantageous alliance.

But it had proved to be a union between two people who really loved each other, and the Dowager Duchess had become a personality in her own right.

There were few people, from the Queen down to the least important employee on the Duke's estate, who did not admire and revere her.

Her hair was dead white and her face was deeply lined, but she still had a beauty which artists wished to project on canvas, and the way in which she held out her blue-veined hands towards her grandson had a grace that was inescapable.

"I heard you were away from home, Durwin," she exclaimed.

"I have returned, and I am extremely glad to find you here, Grandmama."

The Earl kissed both her hands, then her cheek, as he asked:

"What brings you to London—as if I did not know?"

"I had to visit the dentist," the Dowager Duchess replied firmly.

"Nonsense, Grandmama! You know as well as I do it is the beginning of the Season and you would not wish to miss the Social Whirl. In fact I have been expecting you for over a fortnight."

"I am too old to be social," the Dowager Duchess said, but her smile belied the words.

"You could not have come at a more opportune moment as far as I am concerned," the Earl said, seating himself in a chair beside her.

He spoke seriously, and his grandmother, taking a glance at him, said:

"You are about to tell me you are engaged to be married. I hope not to one of those importunate widows who have been besieging you so ardently?"

"No, Grandmama," the Earl replied quickly. "I am not engaged to be married and have no wish to be leg-shackled to any widow, or to any other woman for that matter."

"You play about with enough of them, from all I hear."

"It would be difficult to prevent you from hearing about my escapades since you hear all the scandal that arises in London whether from Carlton House or elsewhere."

"Carlton House!"

The Dowager Duchess's tone of voice spoke volumes.

"There is something I want to tell you," the Earl said quickly, knowing that if his grandmother started on the subject of the Prince Regent it would be difficult to divert her from it.

"What is it?"

"I have discovered by chance that I have been exceedingly remiss regarding a Ward who was entrusted to my care," the Earl explained.

"A Ward?" the Dowager Duchess exclaimed. "I had no idea that you were ever placed in a position of a Guardian. I remember my poor husband . . ."

"I am sure Grandpapa was acutely aware of his responsibilities," the Earl interrupted, "but unfortunately, mine were forgotten until today."

"What happened today?" the Dowager Duchess enquired curiously.

"I met my Ward by chance," the Earl said, "and have brought her with me to London."

"So it is a female!" the Dowager Duchess exclaimed with the air of someone making an unusual discovery. "And I suppose having thrust herself upon you she is now concerned with trying to get you up the aisle."

The Earl laughed.

"On the contrary, Grandmama. She is determined to marry no-one."

"To marry no-one? Can there be such a girl alive who has no wish to capture a husband, and, if possible, you?"

"You must meet Petrina. Incidentally, she is an heiress, so there is no immediate haste for her to get married."

"Are you telling me you have brought this girl here?" the Dowager Duchess enquired.

"For you to chaperon, Grandmama, at least for tonight."

"It is my belief that you have got touched in the head since you have been away," the Dowager Duchess said. "A girl in Staverton House? I have never heard of such a thing before!"

"Nor have I," the Earl admitted ruefully, "but as her father and mother are dead and she has run away from School, there is really no-one else to whom she can turn."

"What does she look like?" the Dowager Duchess

asked suspiciously. "If you think I am going to chaperon some hoyden of a country chit with no countenance and less breeding, you are much mistaken!"

"She is pretty, and her father was Major Maurice Lyndon, who was in my Regiment."

"Lucky Lyndon?"

"You have heard of him?"

"Of course I have heard of him!" the Dowager Duchess answered. "You were either too young to remember, or you were not interested, but your cousin, Gervaise Cunningham, called him out."

"They fought a duel?"

"They certainly did!" the Dowager Duchess replied. "With his usual luck, Lyndon winged poor Gervaise, although the duel was entirely his fault for having been caught in the most compromising circumstances with his wife, Caroline."

"I must admit that if I ever knew of the episode I had forgotten it," the Earl said.

"Caroline was only one of the women who was infatuated with Maurice Lyndon and of course his immense fortune."

"How did he make it?"

The Dowager Duchess threw out her hands in an expressive gesture.

"Gambling, but not with cards—with shares, ships, and property in various parts of the world. I believe, also, he once won a French lottery worth millions of francs."

"As you know so much about him, you will certainly find his daughter interesting," the Earl said. "But I do beg of you, Grandmama, not to tell her too many of her father's exploits. She is already overeager to experience her own!"

"Surely she is too young to have had much opportunity to do anything reprehensible, as she has been at School."

"You would be surprised!" the Earl replied enig-
matically.

He rose and went from the room to fetch Petrina.

While he was with his grandmother, Petrina had
taken off her bonnet and the short jacket she had
worn over her plain schoolgirl's dress.

She should have looked very young and very unsophisticated, but perhaps it was the fiery gold in her
hair, the mischievous glint in her slanting eyes, and
the mocking curl of her lips which gave the Earl the
impression of somebody who should be watched for
fear of what she might do next.

"My grandmother has agreed to chaperon you for
the moment," he said severely as they walked up the
stairs side by side, "and if you make yourself pleasant
to her there is nobody who could give you a better
entrée to the Social World."

"What you are really telling me is that I must be
careful of what I say," Petrina answered.

"And of how you behave!" the Earl added.

She looked up at him, her eyes dancing.

"I have a feeling you are quite nervous about me."

"I certainly have no wish for you to bring disgrace
upon your own head or on mine because I am in
the unfortunate position of being your Guardian."

"I dare say you will quite enjoy it when you get
used to me," Petrina replied. "Besides, I can see
already that you sit here in your grandeur with nothing to think about except your own consequence. It
is time somebody woke you up."

"I have no wish to be woken up, if you mean that
I shall have to spend my time extracting you from
some scrape or other," the Earl said severely. "And
let me inform you, Petrina, that I have the power and
the authority to send you to Harrogate whether you
like it or not, if you misbehave."

Petrina made a little grimace.

"The iron-handed Guardian speaks!" she jeered. "But do not fuss yourself. I shall do my very best to keep out of your way."

"I wish I could be sure of that," the Earl retorted, and heard her chuckle as he opened the door into his grandmother's room.

* * *

Rising early because she found it hard even after late nights to sleep until the fashionable hours of the morning, Petrina went to her bed-room window and saw the Earl riding down the short drive.

She had learnt that he was always up early, riding in the Park before it became crowded, and she wished as she had wished a dozen times before that he would ask her to go with him.

She wondered if he met some entrancing and alluring lady on his rides, or if he preferred to be alone at such an early hour.

Petrina had learnt a great deal about the Earl since she had come to London.

First of all, her friend Claire, whom she had contacted the day after she arrived, had been overwhelmed at hearing where she was staying and who was her Guardian.

"Why did you not tell me about the Earl?" she asked.

"I was ashamed of having a Guardian who paid no attention to me," Petrina replied, "and I hated him because I assumed he was old, strait-laced, and disagreeable."

"Now you find he is none of those things," Claire said. "Oh, Petrina, how much I envy you! I have always longed to meet the Earl, but of course it is well known that he never speaks to unmarried women."

"He has to speak to me."

Petrina was not prepared to acknowledge to her friend that since she had arrived at Staverton House she had had no private conversation with its owner and had only seen him at dinner-parties at the other end of the table.

From the moment she had arrived her days had been occupied with shopping.

She had found that the Dowager Duchess not only enjoyed visiting the most expensive dressmakers in Bond Street, but also had very positive ideas on how her charge was to be dressed if she was to capture the attention of the *Beau Monde*.

At first Petrina had been suspicious that she might be fobbed off with "young girl" gowns, which would make her look insignificant or exactly like every other débutante of the Season.

But to her delight she discovered that the Dowager Duchess, having had herself to achieve success by her personal appearance rather than through her antecedents, knew exactly how to be noticeable without exceeding the bounds of good taste.

It was the Dowager Duchess, Petrina found, who ensured that she was a sensation from the moment she entered a Ball-Room.

She had had no idea before that her hair could look like a flaming torch on top of her well-shaped head, or that with a touch of cosmetics her skin could be almost dazzlingly white and her eyes so large that they seemed to fill her small face.

What was more, although she hardly dared to say it aloud, she had never envisaged while wearing the dull and shapeless clothes that Cousin Adelaide had chosen for her that underneath them she had an exquisite figure.

It proclaimed itself in no uncertain terms once she was dressed by the creative hands of a French dressmaker.

"I was very proud of you tonight, my dear," the Dowager Duchess said after Petrina had been an undeniable success at a Ball given by the Duchess of Bedford.

"It is all due to you," Petrina replied simply.

"You pay for dressing, and at least you have something to say for yourself. I could never abide the type of young girl who simpers or is too shy to raise her eyes from her slippers."

Petrina laughed.

"According to my Guardian, I am not too shy but too forward. I know he is terrified of what I will say next."

Even as she spoke she realised that he was not likely to hear what she said anyway.

Although he had escorted them to several Balls he had not asked her to dance, and she had noticed that his partners were exactly the sort of attractive, sophisticated women she had expected.

It was Claire who had enlightened her further on that score.

"The Earl has been infatuated for nearly a year with Lady Isolda Herbert. She was widowed in the war when she was very young and has been a reigning beauty ever since."

"Do you think the Earl will marry her?" Petrina enquired.

Claire shrugged her shoulders.

"Who knows? Everybody has tried hard enough to catch him, but they say his love-affairs never last long. He finds women a bore once he knows them well."

"Did your brother Rupert tell you that?" Petrina asked.

"Oh, Rupert had a lot to say once I asked him about the Earl. His mistress is an alluring creature. I think Rupert rather fancied her himself but was unable to afford her."

"Who is she?"

"Her name is Yvonne Vouvray. She is a singer at Vauxhall Gardens."

"I should like to hear her," Petrina said.

"I doubt if the Dowager Duchess will let you go to Vauxhall," Claire answered. "It is considered definitely 'out of bounds' for débutantes. But perhaps Rupert and I could smuggle you in one evening and no-one will know anything about it."

"Please try!" Petrina begged.

She was extremely curious to see what the Earl's mistress looked like, but she suspected, having seen Lady Isolda, that she would have dark hair.

The fashion for fair hair and blue eyes, which had been exemplified by the Duchess of Devonshire, had rather petered out, and now brunettes were the rage, especially if they looked like Lady Isolda.

Her jet-black hair, which reminded Petrina of the Earl's horses, her winged eye-brows, and her eyes, which had almost a purple tinge, were framed by the magnificent rubies, emeralds, or opals that she wore in the evening, and gowns which embraced the whole spectrum of the rainbow.

"What are you thinking about?" Claire had asked Petrina yesterday when she had come for tea.

They were alone because the Dowager Duchess, having spent many hours in the shops, had gone to her own room to rest, and the two girls were having tea in the Small Drawing-Room, which Petrina had decided was one of the loveliest rooms in the whole house.

"I was thinking of Lady Isolda, as a matter of fact," she replied to her friend's question.

"You met her last night."

"How did you know?"

"I saw you arrive at the Ball and she was in your party. Did you speak to her?"

"She gave me two cold fingers and looked down her aristocratic nose at me," Petrina replied.

"You only got that because you are staying at Staverton House," Claire said. "I have met her half a dozen times and she has never recognised me so far."

Petrina laughed.

"She is top-lofty like my Guardian. Perhaps that is why he likes her."

Claire looked over her shoulder as if she was afraid someone might be listening, then in a low voice she said:

"Rupert says she is known as a tigress in the Clubs!"

"A tigress? Why?"

"Because she is so fierce and passionate."

"She does not look like that to me."

"That is what is so clever about her. She looks cold and disdainful, until she is alone with a man she likes."

"As she likes . . . the Earl," Petrina murmured.

"Rupert says the betting now is that he will marry her. Everybody is talking about their liaison and sooner or later he will be forced into it."

"That seems to be rather a depressing way of getting married."

Claire laughed.

"I told you, if you want to get a man you have to hand-cuff and drag him with you up the aisle. They are all reluctant husbands."

She saw the expression in Petrina's eyes and laughed.

"You are different, as you well know. You are an heiress. Rupert says all the Beaux are talking about your attractions, which include your bank balance."

"I rather guessed that," Petrina replied.

* * *

Petrina walked into Staverton House following the Dowager Duchess, who moved slowly owing to rheumatism in one of her legs.

The Major Domo bowed to them in his usual obsequious way, and then, as the Dowager Duchess started to mount the stairs, he said to Petrina:

"His Lordship would like a word with you in the Study, Miss."

Petrina felt a sudden feeling of excitement. It was the first time in the two weeks she had been at Staverton House that the Earl had wanted to see her.

She managed to walk demurely behind the Major Domo, although she was longing to run in front of him.

He opened a gold and mahogany door and announced:

"Miss Lyndon, M'Lord!"

The Earl was seated writing at a desk in the centre of the room.

He rose to his feet as Petrina came towards him and she thought that nobody could look more impressive or at the same time so exquisitely garbed.

Other men seemed self-conscious about their clothes when they were as well-cut and elegant as those worn by the Earl, but his seemed to sit comfortably upon him with a casualness that was as obvious as the usual expression of boredom on his face.

He did not appear particularly bored at the moment and she thought he looked at her sharply as if to find fault in her appearance.

She was not in the least worried on that score, however, for she knew that her gown of pale daffodil echoed the lights in her hair and the small necklace of topazes round her neck which came from the Staverton collection was in perfect good taste.

She curtseyed and the Earl gave her a perfunctory bow before he said:

"Sit down, Petrina, I want to talk to you."

"What have I done now?"

"I have a feeling that what you really mean is, what have you done that I have found out about," the Earl replied.

"You are making me feel exactly as if I had been sent for by the Headmistress," Petrina complained. "I may inform you, if you do not know it already, that I have been a model of discretion and decorum. Your grandmother is very pleased with me and so should you be."

"Then why are you on the defensive?" the Earl asked with a hint of amusement in his voice.

"What do you do every day?" Petrina asked impulsively. "I know you go riding in the morning and sometimes we see you at the Balls in the evening, but you seem to have a lot to occupy you."

"As I told you before you came here, I have an extremely well-organised life," the Earl replied, "and I have no wish to change the tenor of my ways."

"I was just curious," Petrina said, "but of course your lady-loves take up a lot of your time."

"I have told you not to speak of such women," the Earl said harshly.

"I was not meaning anything improper," Petrina replied, wide-eyed. "I was in fact speaking of Lady Isolda. Are you going to marry her?"

The Earl brought his clenched fist down on his desk with considerable force.

"I have not brought you here to discuss my private life," he said angrily. "Will you learn, once and for all, Petrina, that is not the way a Ward should speak to her Guardian nor a débutante to anyone."

Petrina gave a rather dramatic sigh.

"You are behaving just as you did when we first met," she said. "I hoped you would be pleased at the exemplary manner in which I have carried out your instructions, but I thought at least where you were concerned I could be myself. However, I see now I was mistaken."

She spoke with affronted dignity and the Earl's lips twisted in a half-smile as he replied:

"I would wish you always to be honest and truthful with me, Petrina, but you know as well as I do that curiosity on a certain subject is barred even when you are talking to me."

"I cannot think why," Petrina replied. "After all, everybody in London is asking if you are going to marry Lady Isolda, and I would feel very foolish if I were to wake up one morning and find it announced in the *Gazette*."

"May I assure you that you have no need to worry on that score," he said. "I have no intention of marrying Lady Isolda, or anyone else for that matter."

He saw a light of triumph in Petrina's eyes and said somewhat ruefully:

"I suppose now you think you have extracted a piece of valuable information from me."

"Well, you must be aware that people are curious about you," Petrina said, "and you are far more interesting to talk about than that red-faced, disgusting, fat, old Regent."

"That is not the way you should refer to your future Monarch," the Earl said reprovingly.

Petrina laughed.

"Now you are being the Headmaster again. 'Yes, Sir, no, Sir, I will be good, Sir!' Why did you send for me?"

The Earl obviously bit back some remark he was going to make about the frivolous manner in which she was speaking to him, and after a moment's pause said:

"I have to inform you that Lord Rowlock has approached me to ask for your hand in marriage. I have informed him that not only would I not give my consent to such an alliance, but he is not to communicate with you in any way in the future, nor, if he does so, are you to speak to him."

"Lord Rowlock? But I find him rather amusing," Petrina replied.

"He is a fortune-hunter of the worst sort," the Earl said. "He has tried for years to marry every young woman who is known to have money. It shows that he needs to have his head examined to have approached me with such a proposition."

"I certainly have no wish to marry him," Petrina said. "But he is more amusing than those beardless boys I am introduced to by every scheming Mama."

"You have my instructions, Petrina," the Earl said. "If Rowlock speaks to you, ignore him; and if he continues to bother you, I will deal with him."

"What will you do?" she asked interestedly.

"There is no need for us to go into details," the Earl replied coldly, "but I can assure you that whatever method I use to get rid of Rowlock will be very effective."

"Would you fight a duel with him?" Petrina enquired. "That would be really exciting! I would love to see you fight someone over me."

"Duelling is forbidden and is out-of-date," the Earl said firmly.

"That is not true," Petrina replied. "Two of Rupert's friends fought a duel only last week in Green Park. He was a Second."

"I am not concerned with the behaviour of young men of Coombe's age who know no better," the Earl said in a lofty tone. "What I am telling you, Petrina, is that you no longer number Lord Rowlock amongst your acquaintances."

"I will consider it," she said provocatively.

"You will do as I tell you or I will send you to Harrogate."

"If you do I will scream all the way from London

to that abominable Spa and I will pay a cartoonist to lampoon you for being so cruel to your poor, defenceless little Ward!"

"You are neither poor nor defenceless," the Earl said, "and as long as you are a guest in my house, Petrina, you will do as I tell you."

"Perhaps I should set up my own establishment," she said in a sweet tone.

He glared at her, then with an effort at self-control he exclaimed:

"You are only trying to provoke me. God, that I should be inflicted with such an abominable brat! Will you behave yourself? If not, I promise you I will make you sorry you were ever born."

Petrina laughed.

"Now you are behaving like a big bad wolf. Your grandmother is doubtless right when she says you have been spoilt ever since you were a child, and I suspect your lady-loves have merely carried on where your Nannies and Governesses left off."

She rose as she spoke and walked towards the door.

As she reached it the Earl stormed at her from his desk:

"You will do as I say, Petrina, or I warn you the consequences will be most unpleasant."

"Woof—woof," replied Petrina, her eyes sparkling. "I adore you when you are fierce and masterful! No wonder you have broken hearts lying round your feet like confetti!"

She left the room, shutting the door behind her before the Earl could speak again, and for a moment he merely glared at the door. Then suddenly, in spite of himself, he began to laugh.

He was well aware that Petrina had been an overnight success, and, although he thought cynically that it was mostly due to the often-exaggerated stories of her fortune, she was nevertheless original and, dressed by his grandmother, undeniably attractive.

There was something lovely as well as mischievous about her face, but he found her extremely exasperating, especially when she defied him. However, he was perceptive enough to realise that most of it was an act put on for his benefit.

"God knows she needs a husband," he told himself, and wondered what sort of man would ever be able to cope with her.

At the same time, he was well aware that his grandmother was delighted with Petrina.

She was not only respectful, considerate, and exceedingly grateful to the older woman, but she was intelligent enough, the Earl found, to have confided in her what the Beaux said to her at the Balls they attended and even to have shown her their love-letters.

Nothing could have amused or interested the Dowager Duchess more.

She loved to be "in the know" about everything and everybody, and it was a long time since she had had such an insight into the behaviour and manners of the younger generation.

"Petrina tells me you have told her to have nothing more to do with Lord Rowlock," she said to the Earl when he went to her Sitting-Room early in the evening.

"He has had the audacity to ask me if he could pay his addresses to Petrina," the Earl said angrily.

"He is certainly a fortune-hunter," the Dowager Duchess remarked. "At the same time, it was unwise of you to forbid Petrina to see him. You know as well as I do that forbidden fruits are always the sweetest."

"Do you mean to say she will defy me?" the Earl asked.

"I would not be surprised," his grandmother replied. "After all, Durwin, you must realise that Petrina is no ordinary, half-witted girl. She has an intelligent and inquisitive mind, which I find exceptionally attractive."

"She is also extremely obstinate," the Earl said harshly.

"Only if you tackle her in the wrong way," the Dowager Duchess replied. "You should have left it to me to tell her to be wary of Lord Rowlock."

"It is not merely a question of being wary," the Earl said angrily. "The damned fellow is a menace! If he cannot get an heiress one way, he will get her another. I am quite convinced he thought Petrina was so young and green that she would not realise what he is like beneath that polished veneer."

"He has wit and is exceptionally good-looking," the Dowager Duchess said. "Both are things which appeal to the very young. Be careful, Durwin, you may drive her into his arms."

"I will see him dead before he marries Petrina!" the Earl retorted.

Because he was so annoyed, he left the room without saying any more.

For a moment there was an expression of surprise in the Dowager Duchess's eyes, then it was replaced by a more speculative look, and there was a faint smile on her thin lips.

* * *

The following morning Petrina called on Claire at her father's house in Hanover Square.

The Marquess of Morecombe was not a rich man although he owned a large estate in Buckinghamshire.

After the splendour of the Earl's residence, Morecombe House seemed shabby, but Petrina, concerned only with Claire, was looking in consternation at her friend's face.

It was obvious that Claire had been crying.

She was pretty in a somewhat insignificant way, with very fair hair and pale blue eyes.

When she was happy she seemed to light up in a manner which quite a number of young men found attractive, but at the moment, with red eyes, she looked, Petrina thought, rather like a flower that had been drenched in a rainstorm.

"What is the matter, dearest?" she asked.

"Oh, Petrina, I am so glad you have come! You must help me ... you must! I do not know what to ... do."

"What has happened?"

"I hardly know how to ... tell you."

"Do not be silly. You know I will help you."

Claire gave a little sob.

"I expected to be able to tell you either today or tomorrow that I was ... engaged."

"To Frederick Broddington?"

"You guessed?" Claire asked.

"As you have talked of no-one else since I came to London, of course I guessed, and I like him very much! You will be very happy, I am sure of it!"

"I would have been ... blissfully happy," Claire said, "but now ... now I cannot marry him ... and, oh, I wish I were dead!"

She burst into a flood of tears which made her last words almost incoherent and yet Petrina heard them.

She moved quickly to Claire's side and kneeling down beside her chair put her arms round her friend.

"It is all right," she said. "I know it will be all right. Tell me what has happened and why you cannot marry Frederick. He is deeply in love with you, he told me so."

"That is what he told me . . . and he saw Papa yesterday . . . who of course gave his . . . consent."

It was unlikely that the Marquess would have done anything else, considering that the Honourable Frederick Broddington was the only son of one of the richest men in England.

Lord Broddington was the owner not only of large parts of London but of valuable building land in Birmingham and Manchester.

He was, moreover, of noble birth, and the basis of his fortune had been founded by his great-grandfather, who had had the vision to buy land on the outskirts of developing towns.

Apart from his wealth, Frederick was just the sort of husband Petrina had thought Claire should have. He was kind and considerate. At the same time, he was intelligent and had decided opinions of his own.

She had liked him and enjoyed talking to him, and she was certain that because he really loved Claire he would make her exceedingly happy in the future.

"What has happened?" Petrina asked now. "Have you quarrelled with Frederick, and if so, why?"

"Of course I have not quarrelled with Frederick," Claire answered through her tears. "It is Sir Mortimer Sneldon who has upset everything . . . Oh, Petrina, why did I ever meet him . . . and why was I such a . . . f-fool?"

"Sir Mortimer Sneldon?" Petrina repeated.

She tried to remember him, then recalled that he was a good-looking, rather dandified Beau whom she had seen at every Ball she had attended, but she had not actually met him.

"Yes . . . Mortimer Sneldon," Claire said. "He asked to be introduced to you, but I refused . . . I was afraid he might . . . hurt you as he has . . . hurt me."

"What has he done?" Petrina asked.

Claire wiped her eyes fiercely with a small, damp handkerchief.

"He is ... blackmailing ... me!"

"Blackmailing you? How can he possibly do that?"

The mere word had brought on Claire's tears again and it was a few seconds before she controlled herself to answer:

"When I ... first came to London he ... flattered me ... and because he was older and very handsome I thought myself ... in love with him."

Petrina's eyes were wide.

"What did you do? How can he blackmail you?"

"I wrote him ... letters ... very stupid letters," Claire said. "You will not understand ... but he was so fascinating, and I think now ... he wanted me to write ... as I did."

"What did you say?"

"How much I loved him ... how I could never love anyone else ... and how I was counting the hours until I ... saw him again."

Claire gave a heart-rending little sob as she went on:

"He kept on saying how much my letters meant to him ... but that he must not ... write any to me because he was afraid Mama might see them."

"How many letters did you write?" Petrina asked.

"I have no idea ... a dozen ... perhaps more ... I cannot remember."

"And when did you give up being fond of him?"

"He gave me up," Claire answered. "He became very enamoured with one of my friends and he ... dropped me ... I was unhappy for a little while ... but then I realised I was lucky to be ... rid of him."

"You certainly were!" Petrina said. "But how can he blackmail you?"

"He learnt that Frederick and I were in love, and

he is demanding that I should buy back the letters which I wrote to him."

"And if you do not . . . ?" Petrina asked.

"Then he will take them to Frederick, and although he knows that Frederick will buy them rather than let him show them round the Clubs . . . which he has threatened to do . . . I know he will stop loving me when he . . . sees what I have written."

Petrina sat back on her heels, thinking.

"How much is he asking?"

For a moment it seemed as if Claire was unable to reply, then through lips that trembled she whispered:

"Five thousand pounds!"

"Five thousand? But that is an enormous sum of money!"

"Sir Mortimer thinks I would be able to obtain a sum like that quite easily once I am married, and he is prepared to wait until I am! But I am to give him a letter promising that he will receive the money within two years . . . otherwise he will go to Frederick!"

"It is the most diabolical thing I have ever heard of!" Petrina cried angrily.

"I know . . . I agree . . . but it is all my fault," Claire said weakly. "You are the only person, Petrina, who can help me . . . please . . . please would you . . . lend me the money?"

"Of course I will, dearest," Petrina agreed, "but before you hand it over so tamely I would like to think about it. I do not see why that man should get away with behaving in such an abominable manner."

"There is nothing else we can do and no-one we can tell. Promise me, Petrina . . . you will not tell anybody!"

Claire's pleading was frantic.

"I promise you," Petrina said, "and I promise too that everything will be all right. Frederick will never know, and you must never, never tell him how foolish you have been."

Claire gave a deep sigh of relief.

"Dearest Petrina, how can I thank you?"

Petrina rose to her feet to walk across the Sitting-Room.

"You can thank me by not worrying any more and forgetting about the whole thing," she said. "It will take me a day or two to get the money—you understand that?"

"You will not tell . . . your Guardian?"

"No, of course not!" Petrina replied. "I will tell nobody, but I want to think."

"About what?"

"About Sir Mortimer Sneldon."

"But . . . why?"

"Because I have a dislike of knowing that the wicked are flourishing like a green bay tree," Petrina said positively.

Claire did not understand, but it did not matter.

She only wiped her eyes again and she moved across the room to put her arms round Petrina.

"Thank you, thank you!" she said. "You are the kindest person in the world and I can never thank you enough."

"And you are going to be the happiest," Petrina said.

"I thought I had . . . lost Frederick," Claire replied. "Oh, Petrina, you do not know how wonderful it is to be in love . . . one day you will feel as I do."

"I very much doubt it," Petrina said, "but I am very, very glad, Claire, that you are happy."

She kissed her friend and left, but as she drove back in the Earl's comfortable carriage to Staverton House she was thinking only of Sir Mortimer Sneldon.

Chapter Three

The Earl retied his cravat with the experienced fingers which always infuriated his valets, who thought themselves indispensable.

As he did so a voice behind him said petulantly:

"Why must you leave? It is still early."

He did not turn to look at Lady Isolda lying on the couch which he had so recently vacated, but after a moment he said:

"I am thinking of your reputation."

There was a hint of laughter in his voice, but Lady Isolda showed she was not amused by replying sharply:

"If you were really concerned about that, you would marry me."

There was a silence while the Earl put the finishing touches to the intricate style of his cravat, which was his own invention.

"We are being talked about, Durwin," Lady Isolda said after a moment.

"You have been talked about, Isolda, ever since you appeared in the Social Sky like a meteor," he replied.

"But where you are concerned it is different."

"Why?"

"Because there is no reason why you should not marry me, and we would make an exceptional and outstandingly handsome couple."

"You flatter me," the Earl remarked mockingly.

Lady Isolda sat up on the couch and pushed the silk cushions behind her back.

"I love you, Durwin!"

"I doubt it," he answered. "To be honest, Isolda, I do not think you have ever loved anybody except yourself."

"That is not true. There is no-one, and this is the truth, no-one who has excited me as you do."

"That is a very different thing," he said. "And it is not always conducive, Isolda, to a happy marriage."

"I do not know what you are talking about," she retorted angrily. "All I know is that you are ruining my reputation and the least you can do is ask me to be your wife."

"The least?" he echoed with raised eye-brows.

She looked up at him and put out her white arms as he stood at the side of the couch.

"Kiss me," she whispered. "Kiss me and let me show you how I need you, and how much you need me."

The Earl shook his head.

"I am going home, Isolda, and you must have your beauty sleep."

"When shall I see you again?"

"Doubtless at some Ball tomorrow night. Is it the Richmonds, the Beauforts, or the Marlboroughs who are giving it? Whoever, it may be, it will be exactly the same as all the others we have attended."

"You know I am not talking about Balls," Lady Isolda said petulantly. "I want to be alone with you, Durwin. I want you to kiss me, to make love to me. I want to be close to you."

It was difficult to understand why the Earl was not moved by the passion underlying her words, the way in which her lips invited his, and the fire behind her half-closed eyes.

He turned away to pick up his evening-coat from the chair on which he had flung it and shrugged himself into it.

He looked resplendent and very elegant; and despite the fact that he had refused her advances and thereby aroused her anger, Lady Isolda could not help thinking that he was the most handsome and attractive man she had ever known.

He was also the most elusive.

Since she had known the Earl intimately Lady Isolda had exerted every wile and every allure in her whole repertoire, which was a very considerable one.

But while it had been quite easy to make him her lover, nothing she could do would make him say the only words she wanted to hear.

As he looked round the room to see if he had forgotten anything—and in the dim light of three candles this was somewhat difficult—Lady Isolda felt as if he was slipping away from her, disappearing into the shadows, and she might never see him again.

As if the thought galvanised her into action, she stepped from the couch.

She ran towards the Earl to fling herself against him, knowing that no other man would be able to resist the softness of her body, the fragrance of the perfume with which her hair was scented, and the passionate demand of her lips.

"I want you. . . I want you, Durwin!" she murmured. "Stay with me, for I cannot bear you to leave me."

Her arms went round his neck but the Earl removed them with some dexterity and picked her up in his arms.

He carried her back to the couch and, throwing her down rather roughly against the satin cushions, said:

"Try to behave yourself, Isolda, until I see you again. If, as you say, people are talking about us, it is more of your making than mine, and you will be the more harmed by it."

This was irrefutably true and Lady Isolda stared up at him to say angrily:

"I hate you, Durwin, when you treat me like a child."

"There is nothing child-like about you, Isolda," the Earl said with a smile. "On the contrary, you are very mature."

He turned as he spoke and walked towards the door.

As it closed behind him Lady Isolda gave a cry of sheer fury, and turning over beat the cushions with her clenched fists.

It was always the same, she thought, with the Earl. He came when it suited him, he left when he wished, and nothing she could say or do made any difference.

Where other men were concerned she was supreme, and they were slaves to her bidding, but the Earl had been her master from the first moment they had met.

"I will make him marry me," she swore from between gritted teeth.

It was an easy thing to say, but the question of how she should do it was a very different matter.

* * *

The Earl let himself out of Lady Isolda's house in Park Street and knew he had only a short distance to walk before he reached Staverton House.

It was convenient, he thought, that he did not have to keep his carriage waiting, thus making his servants aware of his movements.

Park Street lay at the back of Staverton House and he had only to traverse the Mews, most of which belonged to him, and enter the garden by a private gate for which he had a key.

It was a fine warm night with a half-moon rising in the sky and it was easy for the Earl to see the way as he walked down the cobbles of the Mews.

He liked the familiar smells of horse-flesh, leather, and hay, and the sounds of the movements of the animals in their stalls.

A road which led into Park Lane divided the Mews and on the other side of it was the wall of his own garden.

He had nearly reached it when ahead of him from a house on the corner there fell from a second-floor window a large object which struck the cobbles with considerable force.

The Earl started, but he was too far away to see exactly what had fallen. Then he raised his eyes to the windows of the house.

To his astonishment, he saw a man climb out of the second-floor window and start with some dexterity to climb down a drain-pipe.

It was quite a hazardous task and the Earl watched with interest the manner in which the thief, for obviously that was what he was, gripped the drain-pipe with his knees and descended slowly and deliberately.

Walking very softly towards the intruder, the Earl waited until the man had actually reached the ground before he put out his hand to grip him by the neck and the wrist.

"I've caught you in the act!" he said aloud. "And I can assure you, my man, that this will cost you a number of years in prison, if you are not hanged for the crime."

His voice seemed to ring out in the silence of the night.

Then the man he was holding, who he now realised by his size was little more than a boy, gave a cry of fear before he began to struggle.

He struggled frantically, trying to free himself from the Earl's grip and kicking at his legs, but his efforts were completely ineffectual and after a moment the Earl said:

"Be still, or I will give you the beating you so richly deserve!"

As he spoke, the boy's efforts to escape from his clutches dislodged his cap, and he saw a glint of golden hair and beneath it a face which made him stare in sheer astonishment.

"Petrina!"

"All right—it's a fair cop!" Petrina replied. "I suppose I have to admit you are too strong for me."

"What the devil do you think you are doing?" the Earl asked furiously.

He was so astounded that for a moment he found it hard to express himself and his voice was almost incoherent.

He relaxed his grip on her as he spoke, and Petrina, shaking herself as if she were a terrier whose fur had been ruffled, picked up her cap from where it had fallen to the ground.

Then she moved towards the box which the Earl had seen thrown from the window.

"It is a good thing this did not hit you," she said.

She picked it up in her arms, and the Earl, with a great effort of self-control, said:

"I want an explanation and it had better be a good one!"

Petrina sighed.

"I suppose I shall have to give it to you, but not here. We must get away."

She glanced up at the window as she spoke as if she half-expected someone to be looking out; but it was in darkness, as were all the other windows on that side of the house.

"Where have you been? Who lives there?" the Earl enquired fiercely.

At the same time, because Petrina seemed to be warning him, he spoke more quietly than he had before.

She did not answer, but carrying the heavy box started to move away.

The Earl, not concealing his exasperation, took it roughly from her.

"I will carry it!"

Then as he took it he gave an exclamation.

"I know whose house that is. It belongs to Mortimer Sneldon!"

His voice was louder, and again looking over her shoulder Petrina said:

"Hush! Do not shout, you might attract attention."

"*I* might attract attention?" the Earl demanded. "And what do you think you are doing?"

"Come on, let us go quickly," Petrina said.

She reached the door into the garden of Staverton House ahead of him and waited in the shadow of it, although the Earl was certain that she too must have a key.

He drew his from his pocket to open the door and she walked in, but as he was carrying the box she waited to close the door behind him.

Now they were under the trees which bordered the high wall enclosing the garden. There was the fragrance of night-scented stock and some of the lower windows in the house cast a golden gleam onto the terrace ahead of them.

The Earl walked a little way across the lawn, then stopped at a seat which stood below the terrace.

"I have no wish for my servants to see you attired in that indecent manner," he said. "We will talk here."

"No-one will see me," Petrina answered. "I slipped downstairs after your grandmother thought I had gone to bed and came out through the Library window."

"Very well," the Earl conceded grudgingly, "we will go back the same way."

He walked ahead of Petrina up the steps and onto the terrace and found as he expected that the Library window was open.

He entered the room and saw that the candles were lit in the sconces. There was a bottle of champagne open in an ice-bucket waiting for his return and a silver covered dish of pâté sandwiches.

The Earl put the box he carried down on a table by the sofa and walked across the room to pour himself a glass of champagne.

He suddenly felt exhausted and it was not only because of the arduous love-making he had experienced with Isolda.

Finding Petrina dressed as a man and descending from a window in Sir Mortimer Sneldon's house made him feel that he was confronted with a problem that was overwhelmingly formidable.

Holding the glass of champagne in his hand, he turned to see that Petrina was standing in the centre of the room, watching him.

She had not replaced her cap and the candlelight accentuated the red of her hair, which the Earl now saw had been swathed tightly round her head.

Dressed in a tight-fitting pair of pantaloons and a short jacket he recognised as one he himself had worn when he was at Eton, she did not look in the least like the boy she pretended to be but very feminine and, he had to admit, very attractive.

The fact, however, that her eyes, worried and apprehensive, seemed to fill her small face, and she was very pale, made him feel exceedingly angry.

"Tell me," he said commandingly, "exactly what

you have been doing and why you were in Sneldon's house—dressed like that."

"I am sorry if it has made you angry," Petrina answered, "but you must admit it was very bad luck that you should have been passing at that particular moment."

"And if I had not been, I presume you think no-one would have known of this outrageous escapade," the Earl said, his voice rising. "Or had Sneldon something to do with it?"

There was something so unpleasant in the way he asked the question that instinctively Petrina's chin rose defensively.

"Sir Mortimer had everything to do with it," she answered, "but not in a way that directly concerns me."

"What is in that box?"

The Earl glanced at the box where he had set it on the table and saw that it was in fact a heavy cash-box of the sort used in offices.

"Do I have to tell you . . . that?" Petrina asked in a low voice.

"You have to tell me everything!" the Earl asserted. "And I can assure you, Petrina, I have no intention of treating your behaviour as anything but a serious affront to my hospitality."

"I am sorry if I have made you angry," Petrina said again.

"What you really mean," the Earl said bitterly, "is that you are sorry I caught you. I suppose you have some good explanation for becoming a thief, although God alone knows what it can be."

She did not answer and after a moment he stormed:

"Come on! Tell me the story and let me hear what devilment you have been up to now!"

"It is not really . . . my secret," Petrina said hesitatingly, "and I ... promised that I would not ... tell you."

"You will tell me, if I have to beat it out of you!" the Earl said grimly. "It is lucky for you that, thinking you were a mere boy, I did not treat you a great deal more roughly."

"It is exceedingly unsporting to hit someone smaller than yourself," Petrina said with a flash of spirit.

"Thieves and burglars receive their just retribution," the Earl retorted. "Now, are you going to tell me what I intend to hear, or do I have to shake it out of you?"

He took a step towards her as if he would put his threat into operation and Petrina said hastily:

"I will tell you, but could I first please have something to drink? I am very thirsty."

The Earl put his own glass down and with tightened lips went back to the grog-tray.

He poured out half a glass of champagne and taking it back to Petrina, who had not moved, put it into her hand.

She took two or three sips and ran her tongue over her lips as if they were dry, before she said:

"I will tell you the truth because I have to, but please, will you promise never to tell a living soul?"

"I make no promises," the Earl replied. "I am not prepared to bargain with you."

"It does not concern me," Petrina said, "but if anything of what I am about to reveal to you was repeated, it could do immeasurable harm and ruin the lives of two people."

There was a note of sincerity in her voice that was unmistakable and the Earl answered:

"I hope I have never done anything to make you think you could not trust me."

Petrina's eyes met his and after a moment she said:

"No ... of course not."

As if she was suddenly conscious of the way in which she was dressed, a faint flush rose in her cheeks, and she walked towards the box to stand beside the table with her hands on it.

"I think this box contains . . . love-letters," she said in a low voice.

"Yours?" the Earl asked, and the question came like a pistol-shot.

Petrina shook her head.

"As I have told you," she answered, "I have never been in love, but a . . . friend of mine thought herself to be . . . in love with Sir Mortimer for a short time. She wrote him some very foolish letters and now he is . . . blackmailing her."

"Blackmailing her?" the Earl ejaculated.

"He has told her that if she does not promise to give him five thousand pounds within two years, he will take the letters to her fiancé, which might prevent the marriage, or to her husband once they are married."

"I always thought Sneldon was an outsider," the Earl said slowly, "but I did not realise he was quite such a cad as that!"

He spoke as if to himself, then in a different tone he asked:

"But what has this to do with you? Why should you interfere?"

"Because although I was quite prepared to pay the five thousand pounds to help my friend, I saw no reason why Sir Mortimer should get away with it," Petrina answered.

Just for a moment it seemed as if the Earl was going to continue to rage at her. Then, as if he could not help it, a faint smile twisted his lips.

He put his hand up to his forehead and sat down in an arm-chair.

"Only you, Petrina, could think of such a solution to the problem."

"No-one would ever have known I had been there if you had not happened to be in the Mews," Petrina said.

"And if it had happened to be someone else," the Earl retorted, "you might have found yourself in front of the Magistrates tomorrow morning, or in an even worse position which I would not wish to describe to you."

Petrina looked at him with curiosity. Then she said:

"Could we open this box and be quite certain that it does contain the letters in question?"

"Why do you think they are there?" the Earl asked.

Petrina moved from the table to the hearth-rug to sit down on it at the Earl's feet.

"I have really been very clever," she said in a tone he knew so well.

"Tell me!" he ordered.

"When Clai... my friend..."

"I had already guessed it was Claire Catterick you were helping," the Earl interposed. "I have just heard that she is engaged to Frederick Broddington."

"All right then—when Claire told me that Sir Mortimer had threatened her, I was determined, if I could, to get back the letters without having to pay for them." Petrina began.

"You would have found it difficult to draw out such a large sum without my being aware of it," the Earl remarked, then added: "Never mind that. Go on with the story."

"So yesterday evening when I saw Sir Mortimer at a Ball, I asked someone to introduce me to him," Petrina continued. "He wanted me to dance and while we were doing so I deliberately looked absent-minded until inevitably he asked me what I was thinking about.

"I gave a little self-conscious laugh. 'You will think it very foolish of me,' I replied, 'but I was thinking how amusing it would be to keep a diary of everything I do and everyone I meet.'

" 'The Diary of the Débutante,' he murmured. 'That is a good idea!'

" 'I am sure it would be very indiscreet, but it would never be published,' I giggled. 'Not until I was too old for it to matter.'

" 'I think it is something you must certainly do,' Sir Mortimer remarked. 'Put everything you think of in it and do not forget the pieces of spicy gossip which will certainly be of interest to posterity, especially if they are about famous people.'

"I had a feeling," Petrina interposed, looking at the Earl, "that he was thinking I might hear and discover things in this house which could be of use to him."

The Earl did not answer and she continued:

" 'Do you think I could do that?' I asked Sir Mortimer with wide eyes.

" 'I am sure, Miss Lyndon, it would be a fascinating document,' he replied. 'Write down everything you think and hear for the next week and then let me see it.'

" 'I could not show it to anyone, for it might be libellous,' I said, 'like some of the things which are said about the Prince Regent in the newspapers.'

" 'I would not let you get into trouble, Miss Lyndon,' he replied in a caressing tone.

"I was silent for a moment or two," Petrina explained, "then he asked, 'What is worrying you now?'

" 'I was just wondering,' I said, 'where I could keep my diary. You know as well as I do that a writing-desk is never safe from the prying eyes of servants, and there is nowhere else.'

" 'What you need is a cash-box,' he answered. 'You

can buy them in Smythsons in Bond Street, with a special key for which there is no replica.'

" 'What a good idea!' I exclaimed. 'Then all I have to do is keep the key safe and nobody else will be able to read what I have written.'

" 'Nobody except me,' Sir Mortimer said. 'You must not forget that I have promised to be your Editor and advisor.'

" 'You are so kind, so very, very kind,' I told him. 'I will start tomorrow.'

" 'You can get your diary as well as the cash-box from Smythsons,' he said.

" 'I shall go there first thing tomorrow morning,' I promised."

Petrina looked at the Earl.

"That was clever of me, was it not?"

"But how did you know where he kept it?" he asked.

"I guessed it would be in his bed-room," Petrina replied. "If he thought the letters from Claire were worth five thousand pounds, he would not risk letting the box lie about in his Sitting Room. I felt sure too he would have it hidden in his wardrobe, or on top of it."

She smiled and added:

"Papa told me once that when book-markers or punters won a lot of money on a race-course they would hide it on the top of the wardrobe in their bed-rooms, where thieves invariably forget to look."

"And was that where it was?" the Earl asked.

"It was where I looked first," Petrina said.

"How did you get in?"

"I was clever about that, too. I guessed that Sir Mortimer would not keep many servants, because if he were rich he would not need to blackmail Claire! So I went to the basement door and looked to see if all the windows were shut and locked."

She smiled.

"That was another thing that Papa was very insistent about, because thieves in towns often get in through the basement windows because the servants, feeling hot and stifled below ground, leave them open."

"You might easily have been caught."

"It was not really very dangerous," Petrina answered. "There were two windows. I could hear a man snoring in one room, and in the next, which I think was a sort of Sitting-Room, the window was half-open."

She lowered her voice dramatically as she said:

"I climbed in, crept along a passage, and found the way to the stairs. It is only a small house."

"Every word you are saying makes me shudder," the Earl exclaimed. "Supposing you had been caught?"

"You would have had to bail me out of prison," Petrina said. "And I expect you would have been able to blackmail Sir Mortimer into not bringing charges against me."

She thought the Earl looked angry and went on quickly:

"I was quite certain that Sir Mortimer was not at home, because he never leaves whatever Ball he is at until the very end, and anyway I made sure that all the rooms were in darkness before I got in through the basement window."

She looked at the box and said triumphantly:

"I found what I was seeking . . . and there it is! Shall we open it?"

As the Earl did not answer she jumped up, lifted the box off the table, and set it down at his feet.

It was substantially made, and while the Earl looked at it calculatingly, Petrina fetched the gold letter-opener from his desk.

"I thought you might be able to prise it open with

this," she said, "or shall I try to find something stronger?"

"You are not to leave the room dressed like that," the Earl said sharply.

"Very well," Petrina agreed meekly, "and if we start with the letter-opener we might be able to use the poker."

It was with some difficulty and at the cost of several bruised fingers and a large number of hastily smothered oaths from the Earl that finally the box was opened.

Petrina pulled back the lid, then gave a little exclamation.

The box was full of letters tied neatly in piles. There were also bills, notes of hand, and a number of IOUs signed with what appeared to be drunken signatures.

The Earl sat back in his chair.

"You have certainly made a haul, Petrina!"

"So many letters!" she exclaimed. "I wonder which are Claire's."

She pulled out quite a number of bundles before she found what she sought.

"These are Claire's," she said triumphantly. "I would know her writing anywhere."

There were at least a dozen letters, she estimated, and some of them looked as if they contained a large number of pages.

Petrina held them in her hand.

"This is all I want," she said. "What do I do with the rest?"

The Earl looked down at the broken cash-box.

"I think, Petrina," he said, "you had better leave the rest to me."

"What are you going to do with them?"

"I will return them anonymously to their rightful owners," he answered, "and they will then be free from Sneldon's clutches. They will none of them ever know the part you have played in rescuing them, but undoubtedly they will be eternally grateful to their unknown benefactor."

"Do you mean to say that Sir Mortimer was black-mailing all these people?" Petrina asked.

"I do not intend to speculate on his nefarious be-haviour," the Earl said loftily, "but I will make quite sure, Petrina, that in the future a large number of distinguished hostesses do not include him on their invitation lists."

"Will you be able to do that?"

"I can do it," the Earl answered, "and I intend to do so."

"Then I am very glad," Petrina said. "His behav-iour is utterly despicable, and poor Claire was desper-ately unhappy."

"Tell her she can show her gratitude best by not telling anyone, least of all Frederick Broddington, what has happened."

"She would not be stupid enough to do that."

"Women enjoy confessing their sins," the Earl said cynically.

"Not Claire. She wants Frederick not only to love her but also to admire her. Anyway, I will make her swear on everything she holds holy to keep silent."

"That is sensible," the Earl approved; then in an-other tone he said, "But there is nothing sensible about your appearance. Go to bed before I become as angry with you as I ought to be!"

Petrina looked at him with a little smile.

"You are not really angry," she said. "And you know as well as I do that it would have been in-furiating to have to pay up."

"Infuriating or not," the Earl said firmly, "in the future, if you have a problem of this sort you will tell me about it. Is that a promise?"

"I am not . . . certain." Petrina hesitated. "To promise you in such a wholesale way would be . . . a leap in the dark."

"You will stop prevaricating!" the Earl roared at her. "Just because I am letting you off lightly this time, I have no intention of allowing you to get into any more scrapes or take such risks in the future."

He thought Petrina intended to argue, but instead she said unexpectedly:

"You have been very kind and helpful and much . . . nicer than I expected. So, if it pleases you, I will promise."

"Without reservation?" he asked suspiciously.

"Without reservation!" Petrina echoed.

But there was a mischievous smile on her lips which he knew so well.

"After all," she added, "there cannot be many Sir Mortimers in the *Beau Monde*."

"You will tell me about every sort and type of problem before you try to tackle it yourself," the Earl said. "And also, Petrina, let me make it clear that I will not have you dressing up in my clothes."

Petrina looked down at her pantaloons as if she had forgotten she was wearing them.

"Did you recognise them?"

"I cannot imagine anyone else in the house is likely to have an Eton jacket," the Earl replied.

"It is very comfortable," Petrina said with a smile. "You cannot imagine how constraining skirts can be."

"That is not going to be an excuse for you to walk about as you are now," the Earl said. "I only hope to God my grandmother does not see you."

"I wish I could tell her the whole story," Petrina said wistfully. "She would so enjoy it!"

This the Earl had to admit was true, but to retrieve his position of authority he merely said:

"Go to bed, you tiresome brat, and do not forget

your promise or it will be Harrogate, or worse, where you are concerned."

Petrina rose to her feet, still holding Claire's letters.

"Good-night, Guardian," she said. "You have really been very kind and civilised over this, and I am grateful, even if you have injured my neck while my wrist will be black and blue."

"Did I really hurt you?" the Earl asked quickly.

"Quite a lot, as it happens," she answered, "and I think you ought to make reparation by taking me riding with you."

"Now I suppose you are blackmailing me!"

"Will you or will you not pay up?"

"All right," he conceded, "but it is not to become a habit. I dislike feminine chatter first thing in the morning."

"I will be as quiet and meek as a little mouse," Petrina promised.

"That is the last thing you are likely to be!" the Earl remarked. "Go to bed and leave me to cope with all this mess."

Petrina looked down at the bundles of letters in the cash-box.

"At least," she said, "you will be able to discover if you have received more ardent and more interesting love-letters yourself than those written to Sir Mortimer."

The Earl looked up at her half-angrily, then realised that once again she was trying to provoke him.

"Go to bed!" he thundered.

He heard her give a little chuckle as she moved across the room towards the door.

* * *

Upstairs in her bed-room, Petrina put the letters in a safe place, then undressed, and having hidden on top of her wardrobe the Earl's clothes, which she had found in a cupboard, she got into bed.

In the darkness she thought over what had happened and decided that on the whole it was a good thing that he had caught her.

Now he could deal with the other letters while she would not have known what to do with them.

At the same time, it had been a moment of sheer terror when she felt him gripping the back of her neck.

Petrina had learnt quite a lot since coming to London and she had known that while she had been in danger of being arrested as a thief she could also have been in a different sort of danger.

There were, she had learnt, Rakes who pursued women in a way that she knew could be very frightening.

Things that were said in conversations she had overheard and that she had read in newspapers had told her a great deal about the world since she had been in London.

She had learnt that there was a great deal of unrest in the country over the restrictions imposed by the Government, the wide-spread poverty, and, above all, the injustices under the law.

The papers which the Earl took reported the political situation, which was something that had never been discussed or even mentioned at Petrina's School.

Now she learnt that petitions for reform bombarded the Regent, in vain.

In Birmingham, she read, a town meeting of at least twenty-five thousand men who had never had a Member of Parliament, and never would if the Government's line held, had elected a radical Baronet as their representative.

The anger of the hundreds and thousands suffering from a renewed trade slump had resulted in penny-a-week Political Clubs. They organised their own reading-rooms and Sunday-Schools.

Parliament had passed, after four years of frustrating argument, an unenforceable act to limit children in the cotton-mills to a twelve-hour day!

Petrina also read, in the more outspoken newspapers, the reports of the social conditions in London and other great cities.

She had a feeling that if the Earl knew how interested she was in what was happening in a very different sphere from the one in which he lived, he would somehow stop the information from reaching her.

So she did not ask for the more scurrilous papers and magazines to which he subscribed, but found that she could obtain them quite easily the day after they were issued.

Then they were taken from the Library and stacked outside his Secretary's office for a week in case they should be required.

It was quite easy for Petrina to make an excuse to visit Mr. Richardson, who kept a safe containing the Staverton jewels in his office and also provided her and the Dowager Duchess with any petty-cash they should require.

After she had left his office she would purloin what newspapers she required from the pile in the passage.

The *Political Register,* which was edited by William Cobbett, was selling fifty thousand copies a week and denounced in no uncertain terms the Government of the day and the lack of interest in the sufferings of the poor, felt by the aristocrats headed by the Prince Regent.

It was the *Political Register* which told Petrina that the Police were ineffective and largely corrupt, and nothing was being done about the Flash Houses where boys were trained as delinquents in their early teens and sent out thieving, picking pockets, and pilfering.

She learnt that when any of these boys was arrested for some minor pilfering, he was sent to prison, flogged, then turned out without a penny in his pocket.

This meant that, unless he was prepared to sleep in sheds and live on garbage, he had to go back to the Flash House where he would find food and warmth if he agreed to return to his criminal activities.

In the *Political Register* there were also reports on the hell endured by the "Climbing Boys" who were sent up chimneys to clean them.

There was an official minimum age of eight, but children of four to six were often used. They were badly fed, had to sleep on a floor, and might go for months covered with soot without being washed.

There were not only the newspapers to teach Petrina about what was happening in the world outside Staverton House.

There were cartoons which everybody bought as a matter of course and discussed with laughter and sometimes a good deal of spite at the parties she attended.

The Prince Regent, depicted as enormously fat, with Lady Hertford, covered with the Royal jewels, sitting on his knee or riding him as if he were a bicycle, would make everybody laugh.

But Petrina felt as if some of the gilt was being rubbed away from the gingerbread of the Social Scene that had at first appeared so attractive.

She wondered why the Earl had been so strait-laced where she was concerned, when it was obvious that all the people he knew from the Prince Regent downwards were behaving in what seemed to her a very reprehensible manner.

At the same time, the great majority of the populace were, if the newspapers were to be believed, suffering from poverty and intolerable conditions in work and housing.

"I do not understand it all," Petrina said to herself.

But she went on reading everything she could and was often tempted to ask the Earl about the things which puzzled her.

Then she told herself he would merely think that she was being tiresomely curious and that it was not her concern.

'But it should concern everybody!' she had thought as she and the Dowager Duchess drove along Piccadilly.

She could see the poverty of the Crossing-Sweepers and the children in rags huddled in doorways, waiting to steal from the more affluent passers-by or hoping someone would take pity on them and toss them a coin.

So much wealth, so much abject misery, and no-one seemed to care. It was all very puzzling! And Petrina told herself she must do something to help.

'I suppose I have now promised the Earl I will not do anything without telling him first,' she thought now as she lay in the darkness.

He was at this moment sorting out the letters that she had stolen from Sir Mortimer.

By doing that she had at least righted one wrong. At the same time, there were so many more injustices and she felt appalled at the difficulties of entering the fray against them.

She gave a little sigh and realised there was nothing she could do except try to work out the solution alone.

The Earl would not understand. He merely thought her a tiresome brat, a child who was playing with fire.

She felt for a moment undeniably childish in wanting his help, in feeling that he was so strong and so all-powerful that he could achieve more than she could ever hope to do.

Then she told herself he was not interested in her problems, but in Lady Isolda Herbert.

She was beautiful, very beautiful, there was no doubt about that!

With a little sinking of her heart which she could not understand, Petrina realised that in comparison with Lady Isolda she must indeed seem a child and very insignificant.

"If he does marry her, as everyone expects," Petrina asked herself, "what will become of me?"

It was a question which made her feel suddenly afraid of the future.

She had thought she would hate living at Staverton House, and yet now she loved it.

It was not only the house, which was so beautiful and its surroundings a joy. It was also exciting, in some way that she could not explain, that the Earl was there.

She might not see him often, but even when he was absent she was vividly conscious of him.

When he came into the Salon before dinner or on rare occasions joined her and his grandmother when they were alone, the tempo seemed to quicken and she felt a strange sensation of excitement creep over her that had not been there before.

Yet she wanted to defy him, to challenge him, to tease him.

It was something she never felt with other men, and yet with the Earl the feeling was inescapable, although she could not explain it.

"Please, God, do not let him get married . . . too quickly," she found herself praying.

It was the most selfish prayer she had ever made.

Chapter Four

The Earl looked up from the newspaper which he was reading to see his Secretary standing just inside the door of the Library.

"What is it, Richardson?" he asked.

"Could I speak to you a moment, My Lord?"

"Of course," the Earl replied, setting down his newspaper. He noted that Mr. Richardson looked worried as he moved across the room towards him.

A middle-aged man, he had been with the Earl's father before him and knew more about the Staverton houses and estates than either of their owners did.

He was tactful with the servants and the other employees and at the same time kept a firm hand on every detail, so that the Earl knew that, unlike what happened in so many aristocratic houses, food was not being sold by his Chefs and his Butlers were not stealing the wine.

"What is worrying you, Richardson?" he asked in a pleasant tone.

There was a moment's pause before Mr. Richardson replied:

"I thought Your Lordship ought to know that Miss

Lyndon is drawing very large sums of money from her account."

"I suppose that is to pay for the gowns and furbelows that are considered necessary for a débutante's Season in London," the Earl remarked.

"No, My Lord, I pay the dressmakers' and milliners' bills and they are not abnormally large."

The Earl's expression changed.

"Are you telling me that Miss Lyndon draws the sums you mention in cash?"

"Yes, My Lord. She tells me what she requires, signs the cheques, and I have the money ready for her the following day."

He thought the Earl looked incredulous as he handed him a piece of paper.

"This is what Miss Lyndon has asked for this last week, My Lord."

The Earl took the paper from him, glanced at it, then said in an ominous tone:

"Is Miss Lyndon in the house?"

"I think, My Lord, she has just returned from riding."

"Then send a footman to say I wish to speak to her immediately."

"Very good, My Lord."

Again there was a pause before Mr. Richardson said:

"I hope I have done right in telling Your Lordship what was occurring. I feel, however wealthy Miss Lyndon may be, this might, if it continues, constitute a considerable drain on her fortune."

He was obviously embarrassed at what he had to say, and the Earl answered reassuringly:

"You have done entirely right, Richardson. I am, as you know, Miss Lyndon's Guardian, and it is I who must make an accounting of her money when it finally passes into her hands."

"Thank you, My Lord."

Mr. Richardson bowed and went from the room, but the Earl, with a frown between his eyes, rose to walk to the window.

"What the devil is Petrina up to now?" he asked himself.

He looked down at the sums of money that Mr. Richardson had inscribed on the piece of paper which he now held in his hand, and his lips tightened.

He had felt certain, after she had given him her promise the night he had caught her robbing Sir Mortimer Sneldon, that she would behave better in the future.

He thought he had obtained not only her promise but also her trust. But now he told himself angrily it was foolish to think that any woman was straight and honest. They all cheated when they got the chance.

On the desk behind him there were two letters from Lady Isolda which he had not yet opened.

Because he had not been to see her for several days she had bombarded him with messages and notes, and he knew that sooner or later he would have to make her face the fact that their liaison was over.

As was inevitable where he was concerned, it was only a question of time before he became bored with any woman, however beautiful she might be, however attractive.

The Earl knew that once something became commonplace it also became banal.

He found that Isolda's conversation bored him and her persistent complaint that he would not marry her made him yawn.

She was not in the least the type of woman with whom he wanted to spend the rest of his life.

He was not quite certain in his own mind what the woman would be like whom he would wish to bear his name and his children.

But he did know for sure that she did not look or behave like Isolda.

He had been involved in too many *affaires de coeur* not to know that when inevitably he tired first, it usually resulted in an extremely unpleasant scene, which, where Isolda was concerned, if he was not careful, would reverberate throughout the whole of the Social World.

"Dammit! Why did I have to get involved with her?" he asked.

He knew the answer was that she had deliberately sought him out and attempted, as so many other women had done, to capture him.

He was, however, concerned at the moment not with Isolda and the problem she presented, but with Petrina.

When a few moments later she came rushing into the room with her usual impetuosity, he turned to look at her and the darkness in his eyes deepened.

"Forgive me for being so long, Guardie," she said, her eyes sparkling, "but I got your message when I was in my bath, and I thought you would wish me to wear something more respectable than a towel before I obeyed your imperial summons."

She moved confidently towards him, looking extremely attractive in a morning-gown of pale blue muslin trimmed with tiny frills round the skirt and narrow velvet ribbons of the same colour.

As the Earl had his back to the light, Petrina had reached his side before she saw the expression on his face.

She looked up at him and for a moment she was still.

"What has happened?"

"I thought I could trust you to keep your word," the Earl said, and his voice was like a whip, "but I see I was mistaken."

"Keep my word?" Petrina questioned. "If you mean my promise to you...I have kept it. I have done nothing reprehensible, I assure you."

"You lie!" the Earl said savagely. "And let me tell you, Petrina, if there is one thing I really dislike and abominate, it is being lied to."

"But . . . I am not lying."

"You are!" he said harshly.

"What have I done?" Petrina asked. "I swear I have no idea of anything I have done wrong."

"You are being blackmailed!"

He saw the astonishment in her face as her eyes widened and she said:

"I swear to you on everything I hold sacred...I am not being blackmailed. And in any case, there is nothing for me to be blackmailed about."

"Then perhaps you will explain this," the Earl said ominously.

He showed her the piece of paper he held in his hand and Petrina looked at it.

She stared down at the sums of money and the colour rose in her cheeks.

The Earl made an exclamation of fury and walked towards the mantelpiece to stand with his back to the empty fireplace.

"Now," he said, "perhaps I may hear the truth."

Petrina gave a little sigh.

"I did think of telling you, but I thought you would not . . . understand."

"Who is the man, and what hold has he over you?"

"There is no man."

"Do you expect me to believe that?"

"It is true!"

"Then to whom have you given these vast sums of money?"

There was a pause, then Petrina said:

"It is . . . my money."

"For which I am responsible until you are twenty-one."

"Perhaps I should have . . . asked you, but I felt you would . . . prevent me from doing what I . . . wanted to do."

"You may be quite sure of that."

"Now you understand why I could not tell you."

"You will tell me now!" the Earl commanded.

Again Petrina hesitated, before she said in a low voice:

"I was going to ask you how I could help these wretched girls, but I felt you would . . . disapprove and . . . stop me. So I thought I could give them money without you . . . knowing about it."

"What girls?" the Earl asked.

"The women . . . in the streets."

The Earl stared at her in astonishment, then he said in a more gentle tone:

"Suppose you start at the beginning? I find it hard to understand what you are trying to tell me."

He sat down as he spoke in one of the arm-chairs by the fireplace and made a gesture with his hand to invite Petrina to occupy the other.

She sat down on the very edge of the chair and her eyes, dark and worried, looked at him apprehensively as if she was sure that he was going to be extremely incensed with her.

"It all started," she said, "one morning when your grandmother was not feeling well, so I went to the shops with Hannah, my lady's-maid.

"When we came out there was a girl with a very young baby in her arms. It was very small and sick-looking. She asked me to help her. I gave her a little money, and as she was so young, I asked if the baby belonged to her."

Petrina gave a quick glance at the Earl as if in embarrassment, then looked away.

"She told me," she went on in a low voice, "that she had only been fourteen when she came to London from the country to get a job. Somehow, I am not certain how it happened, she was picked up at the Coach-Station by a man who said he would ... help her."

Petrina's voice was even lower as she went on:

"He gave her a lot of gin to drink. She was not ... certain what ... happened afterwards, but she never ... saw him again."

"This sort of thing does occur when girls come to London alone," the Earl said dryly.

"Ethel ... that was her name ... managed to get some work, but when she found she was having a baby they dismissed her."

Petrina's voice faltered as she said:

"She said the only thing ... she could ... do was to ... become a ... prostitute."

There was an uncomfortable silence and as the Earl did not speak she went on:

"Then after she had the baby she had to beg to keep them both alive."

"She told you this story while you stood talking to her in the street?" the Earl questioned.

"We were not in Bond Street, but in Maddox Street where it is not so crowded," Petrina explained, "and I was so sorry for her. I gave her all the money I had with me and went back the next day to give her more, but I could not find her."

The Earl made a restless sound and Petrina continued quickly:

"I could not sleep that night thinking how thin and ill she looked and how small and sick the baby was."

"That accounts for some of the money you have spent," the Earl remarked, "but what about the rest"

"When I drove about London with your grandmother," Petrina answered, "I could see the children

in rags and the girls with painted faces and gaudy cloth-
ing waiting to ... speak to ... gentlemen passing by."

"You should not notice such things," the Earl said
sharply.

"How could I help it, unless I were blind?" Petrina
replied.

Her retort held a touch of the old spirit in her
voice. Then as if she was afraid to anger him more, she
went on in a quieter tone:

"I have read about the conditions of women and
young girls in London, of the ... prostitution in the
streets and the way they are ... exploited by people
who keep them in a state of slavery."

"That is not suitable reading for you," the Earl remarked. "Where can you have obtained such litera-
ture?"

Petrina did not answer and he said insistently:

"I asked you a question. Where have you read of
such things?"

"In the newspapers and magazines you have here."

"They were not intended for your eyes."

"I think it is right that I should know the state of
London at this moment," Petrina said, "and it is not
only the *Political Register* which writes about such
things, there have also been speeches in the House
of Commons on the subject."

The Earl was aware of this, knowing that there had
been a large number of debates on the findings of a
Select Committee set up the previous year to investi-
gate these actual conditions.

Members of the Police Force who were not dishonest
had given evidence, and the Members of Parliament
had been astounded and shocked by what they learnt.

But while the Earl and a great many other men had
discussed and debated the findings, there was not one
lady of his acquaintance who had been the slightest bit
interested.

He was astounded now at what Petrina was saying, but aloud he merely said:

"I want to know to whom else you have given money."

"I am afraid perhaps you will be angry with me," Petrina replied, "but one evening after I had met Ethel I . . . walked down Piccadilly to see for . . . myself what was happening."

"You *walked* down Piccadilly?" the Earl ejaculated. "Alone?"

"No, not alone," Petrina answered. "I am not as foolish as that! I left the carriage at the end of Bond Street and made Jim the footman walk with me."

"Jim had no right to do anything of the sort!" the Earl thundered.

"You must not be angry with him," Petrina said quickly. "I forced him to do so, I said that if he would not accompany me then I would go by myself."

The Earl opened his lips to rage at her, then controlled himself and merely asked:

"What happened?"

"I talked to quite a number of women, one or two of whom were rude, but the others when they realised I wanted to help them answered my questions and told me how they had started on the life they now lead."

"And you gave them money?"

"Of course! And most of them were very grateful. They said it meant that they could have a night off and go home early to bed."

The Earl doubted that this would happen and was sure that the money had been taken from them by their procurers, who invariably had them watched.

Though he did not say this aloud, Petrina went on:

"One of the girls told me, which I did not know before, that she would not be allowed to keep the money herself and so I arranged for her to meet me the next morning in the Park. Afterwards I did that with quite a lot of them."

The Earl put his hand up to his forehead as if to iron away the lines of perplexity between his eyes.

He was quite certain that Petrina would not have succeeded in helping the wretched prostitutes at all, as she hoped she was doing.

The procurers, male and female, kept a very sharp eye on the women who brought them enough money to keep carriages and own villas in respectable suburbs.

He remembered someone in the House of Commons saying there was no record of even one of these harpies being carted off to gaol.

They were the owners of the brothels and also of the wretched creatures who walked the streets usually in a state of intoxication.

They handed over their pitiable earnings in return for a roof over their heads until they were too unattractive or too disease-ridden to continue their nefarious trade.

"I helped the women in Piccadilly," Petrina was saying, "but I wanted most of all to help those with children. They now recognise the carriage when it appears in Bond Street and there are usually two or three waiting for me."

She glanced at the Earl nervously as she explained:

"As your grandmother, if she is with me, gets into the carriage, I have little packets of money ready to put in their hands."

She looked at him with beseeching eyes as she said:

"I am afraid I have spent rather a lot, but every time I put on a pretty gown or wear some of the wonderful jewellery from your collection, I cannot help thinking how those poor women have to earn money and how many children go hungry."

There was a little sob in Petrina's voice and suddenly her eyes were full of tears.

She jumped up from the chair to walk to the window so that the Earl should not see her crying.

He watched her silhouetted against the sunlight, which turned her hair into a halo of gold. Then he said quietly:

"Come and sit down, Petrina. I want to talk to you about this."

She wiped her eyes surreptitiously, then did as he told her, returning to the chair she had just vacated.

"I understand your feelings," the Earl said, "but I wish you had trusted me and told me how deeply you felt about these women."

"I thought you would stop me," Petrina answered. "Papa always said it was throwing away good money to give it to beggars, but I . . . *had* to help them."

"I can understand your wishing to do so, but in the future it must be in a more practical manner."

Petrina looked at him.

"I was thinking," she said slowly, "that when I am twenty-one and have my own money I could build a home or a hostel where these women could take their babies for food and shelter."

"That is a very good idea," the Earl answered.

He did not wish to disillusion her by explaining that many of the babies she thought she was helping were merely hired out for the day, passing from one woman to another and used only as a method of evoking charity from those who had a soft heart.

"Do you mean you would help me?" Petrina asked.

"I will certainly advise you how to give your money to charity in a reasonable and sensible manner."

"I want to help the girls like Ethel who have a baby by . . . mistake when they are not married."

"That should not be difficult," the Earl answered. "There is, as a matter of fact, I believe, some assistance being given already to unmarried mothers."

"There is?" Petrina asked. "There does not seem to be much sign of it."

"That is true," the Earl agreed.

He knew that Petrina had no idea of the magnitude of the problem which she had stumbled upon by accident, or perhaps it was because she was more sensitive than other women in the *Beau Monde*.

"I think you will find," he said, "that Churches like St. James's in Piccadilly are well aware that these women, especially those with children, need help. I think the best thing you can do at the moment, Petrina, is to discuss this matter with the Vicar."

He saw that she was not very enthusiastic about the idea and added:

"I am quite sure you will find that the reason his work is not more extensive is simply lack of funds."

"Then I can give him some of my money."

Petrina's voice was suddenly breathless.

"Certainly," the Earl agreed, "as long as you discuss it with me first, and we are both convinced it will be put to the very best possible use."

"Oh, thank you, thank you!"

"It is your money, not mine."

"I want to help! I want so much to do something really good with my fortune," Petrina said, "but what I cannot understand . . ."

She stopped as if she thought what she was about to say might be embarrassing.

"What can you not understand?" the Earl asked.

"Why must there be so many women walking about the streets or so many men . . . interested in them?"

She was thinking as she spoke of how coarse and common many of the women were, especially those who had been rude to her.

Although she had walked down Piccadilly very early in the evening there had been a surprising number of young girls who were so drunk they could hardly stand.

It had been an eye-opener and at the same time a shock, and Petrina knew she would never forget what she had seen or how pitiful were the stories she had been told.

As if he knew what she was thinking, the Earl, watching her, said:

"It takes time to reform the world, Petrina, and it is not possible for one person to do it alone."

"I know that," she answered, "but you have so much power and authority. You can speak in the House of Lords, you can influence the Regent."

The Earl smiled.

"You are crediting me with powers I do not possess!" he protested. "But I have, as it happens, already spoken on this subject in the Lords and I am quite prepared to do so again."

"Will you? Will you really?" Petrina asked. "What they want is help, not laws which will only result in their being taken to prison."

"You have put your finger on one of the greatest difficulties we have come up against so far," the Earl said. "At the same time, Petrina, may I suggest that your interest in these women is not compatible with your being a débutante."

He spoke kindly and once again Petrina rose from the chair and walked across the room to the window.

She stood looking out onto the garden in silence, then said:

"You must have been . . . laughing at me when I told you what I . . . intended to be when I . . . came to London!"

The Earl smiled. He could still hear Petrina's voice telling him defiantly that she intended to be a Lady-Bird.

"I told you you did not understand what you were saying," he replied.

"I am . . . ashamed," she answered. "Ashamed not

only of what I said, but because I thought it was an amusing way of living and not the . . . horror and . . . degradation it actually is."

He knew by the way she spoke that she had been shocked and appalled by what she had seen, and he told himself angrily it was something that should never have happened.

"Come here, Petrina," he said.

She did not obey him and after a moment he rose and walked across the room to stand beside her.

"I am going to give you a word of advice," he said. "I doubt if you will take it, but it is something every reformer has to learn sooner or later."

"What is that?"

"You must not become too involved personally and emotionally with the people you are trying to help."

He saw the protest in her eyes before he added:

"If you tear your heart in pieces, all that will happen is that you will become a fanatic. You will lack the balanced and sensible outlook which is essential for any work you may wish to do, in whatever field it may be."

Petrina thought this over for a minute, then she said:

"I can understand that, and you are right. But, oh, Guardie, I cannot bear to think of those very young girls and . . . why are the . . . men whom they wait for not . . . sorry for them?"

"If you want me to help you on this project," the Earl said, "I think we have to approach it from a different angle. If it pleases you, we will go tomorrow to see the Vicar of St. James's in Piccadilly. You can find out what he is doing to help these unfortunate women, and I am quite certain he will welcome wholeheartedly any financial assistance you can give him."

"You will really come with me?" Petrina asked.

"On one condition."

She looked up at him apprehensively.

"It is that you make no further personal investigations," he said, "and incidentally, that is not a request —it is an order!"

"I knew you would stop me."

"For the best of reasons," he answered. "First, because you will be imposed upon, and secondly, this is not a subject that should concern a lady."

"Then it should be!" Petrina said fiercely. "Every woman should know what other women have to suffer, especially when they are too young and too inexperienced to look after themselves."

"That might apply to you," the Earl said quietly.

She gave him a rueful smile.

"I might have guessed you would take up that point, but after all, I have you to look after me."

"When you allow me to."

"I am sorry now that I did not tell you at once," Petrina said, "but you were so positive in telling me I should not speak even to you on that subject."

"I might have known you would find an extenuating excuse for your behaviour!" the Earl remarked.

"I want you to help me," Petrina cried, "I want it very much! It would be so marvellous, more marvellous than I can possibly tell you, if we could do it . . . together."

She put out her hand as she spoke and slipped it in his.

"I never thought you would understand," she went on in a low voice, "but you do, and that makes me feel that everything will be all right."

She felt the strength of the Earl's fingers holding hers, then she added:

"You will not tell your grandmother that I . . . deceived her when I walked down Piccadilly with Jim? She thought I was with Claire."

"I promise that everything you have told me will be in confidence."

She smiled at the Earl but her eyes were misty again.

"You are wonderful!" she exclaimed. "Really wonderful!" And I promise to be very good in the future."

"I very much doubt it," the Earl said, but he was smiling as he spoke.

* * *

Petrina looked round her with excitement.

The famous Gardens at Vauxhall were exactly as she had expected them to be, but the lights seemed more vivid and the supper arrangements more amusing than she could have imagined.

She had a pang of conscience when she was dressing for dinner because she was deceiving the Dowager Duchess and therefore incidentally the Earl, but she told herself that it would have been impossible to disappoint Claire after she had gone to so much trouble to arrange the evening.

She had been so grateful to Petrina for getting back her letters that she had longed to show her gratitude by doing something that she knew would please her.

When Petrina had put the pile of letters into her hands, Claire had burst into tears.

"Petrina, my letters! How can I ever thank you?" she sobbed.

Then through her tears she had cried:

"I will pay you back. You know I will pay you back, although it may take a long time."

"You do not owe me one penny," Petrina said.

Claire's tears had ceased through sheer astonishment.

"It is true," Petrina went on.

"B-but . . . how . . . I do not understand. . . " Claire

stammered. "He could not have ... g-given them to you."

"I stole them!" Petrina told her. "But you must never tell anyone. You must swear to me, Claire, that you will never tell anyone about the letters or how I obtained them."

"I swear ... of course I swear!" Claire agreed. "Tell me ... tell me what happened."

When she heard the whole story she was stunned.

"How could you have been so brave? How could you have done anything that was so dangerous for me?"

"Because you are my friend, Claire, and because I think Sir Mortimer is utterly despicable. I could not bear him to gain so much money in such a disgraceful manner."

Claire looked at her in astonished admiration. Then they had burnt the letters together, burnt them carefully in the grate until every scrap of paper had become nothing but a black ash.

As the flames flickered out, Claire gave a deep sigh of relief.

"Now Frederick will never know."

"Never ... unless you tell him ... and that you must never do," Petrina said.

"I have promised you, Petrina," Claire replied solemnly, "and I will not break my promise."

She had kissed Petrina, thanking her again and again, but ever since then she had been trying to find a way to reward her.

Petrina knew when Claire said she had arranged supper at Vauxhall that it was a celebration which only they could appreciate.

They had dined first at Claire's house with both the Marquess and the Marchioness of Morecombe, which made the conversation rather stilted.

However, when the older people thought they were

going to a Ball, Claire and Petrina, accompanied by Frederick Broddington and Viscount Coombe, had set off for Vauxhall Gardens.

It had, despite its somewhat doubtful reputation, the seal of respectability in that the Prince Regent, who often went there, had his own Pavilion with its private entrance to the road.

But because it was a public place, it was also thronged with anyone who was prepared to pay the entrance fee.

Petrina was warned that there were pick-pockets amongst the crowds, the majority of whom looked well dressed and prosperous as they perambulated beneath the trees.

The two gentlemen hurried the girls along the crowded paths to the Rotunda, where supper was served in the small alcoves which faced it in a semi-circle and were furnished in Eastern style.

Each alcove which was used as a supper-box was decorated with paintings, and the one in which Petrina found herself was called "the Dragon."

It depicted a fire-breathing green monster which the Viscount Coombe declared had "an expression on its face exactly like the Prince Regent's when Parliament refused to vote him any more money."

Petrina found Claire's brother rather disappointing. He was certainly, as his sister had described him, a "Tulip of Fashion," but he also affected the languid air, the drooping eye-lids, and the bored voice of the "Dandy Set," which she found irritating.

He was very different from Frederick Broddington, whom she liked more every time she met him.

But it was obvious he had eyes only for Claire, and Petrina realised she was expected to make herself pleasant to the Viscount and try to engage him in polite conversation.

He was however somewhat difficult to converse

with, and she had the uncomfortable feeling that he had been pressured by his sister to make a four this evening and would have much preferred to be elsewhere.

However, he answered some of her questions and ordered them slices of the famous Vauxhall ham which cost an outrageous price and also champagne, which was not, Petrina realised, of the same quality as the champagne she had drunk at Staverton House.

She looked wide-eyed at the Rotunda where she was told there were Hogarth's pictures of Henry VIII and Anne Boleyn.

From the supper-box she could see the ornate double-fronted Band-Stand, which looked like a Chinese Pagoda although it was surmounted by the Prince of Wales's feathers.

The Musicians were playing and some of the people were dancing, but the majority were just wandering round, staring at one another in the light of the five thousand oil-lamps which made Vauxhall undoubtedly one of the brightest places in London.

"What time does the entertainment start?" Petrina asked the Viscount.

"It should not be long now," he answered, "but I will go and find out."

He rose and left the supper-box with an alacrity which made Petrina think that he had other reasons for wishing to be on his own. But she did not miss him, much preferring to watch the crowds moving in front of her.

Frederick Broddington was obviously whispering words of love to Claire, who with flushed cheeks was looking very pretty and very happy.

Petrina moved her chair as far away as she could to the other side of the supper-box so that she should not even inadvertently hear what they were saying to each other.

It was then that, from the other side of the partition which divided them from the alcove next door, she heard a voice she recognised say:

"She not only sings divinely but is exceptionally seductive, as the noble Earl certainly appreciates."

"I curse him every day for having beaten me to the post!" a man's voice replied.

"You are boasting, Ranelagh," the first man said with a laugh, and Petrina knew that the voice belonged to Lord Rowlock.

She was aware now to whom he was speaking, for she had met the Duke of Ranelagh at one of the Balls she had attended and had danced with him.

She had thought him a boastful, conceited young man and he had made it obvious that he was not particularly interested in her.

"I hear that Staverton has bought Yvonne a house in Paradise Row in Chelsea, and set her up with a carriage which knocks spots off all the horses of the *Ton*," Lord Rowlock continued.

"I have not only heard about the house, I have been there!" the Duke replied.

"Good heavens!" Lord Rowlock exclaimed. "Did you crawl through the key-hole? I cannot believe the Earl took you on a tour of inspection."

"I am not without my resources," the Duke said boastfully, "and to tell the truth, Rowlock, our French charmer has made no bones about the fact that she fancies me."

Lord Rowlock did not reply and the Duke went on:

"But I was frank. I told her I was not deep in the pocket like Staverton and we have come to a very amicable arrangement.'"

"What sort of arrangement?" Lord Rowlock asked.

Petrina could not see the Duke, but she had the feeling that he was looking smug and pleased with himself, and she was sure that he winked at his friend.

"When the cat's away, the mice will play," he said evasively.

"What do you mean by that?" Lord Rowlock enquired.

"You can guess," the Duke answered. "Staverton is not always in London, nor, when he is with the demanding Lady Isolda, is he in Chelsea."

"Do you mean . . . ? Lord Rowlock ejaculated.

"I mean I am very much *persona grata* with our little French Love-Bird," the Duke replied.

Lord Rowlock gave an exclamation.

"For God's sake, man, be careful what you do where Staverton is concerned. He is a dead shot and I am quite certain would allow nobody, least of all you, to poach on his preserves."

"I am discretion itself, my dear fellow," the Duke said airily, "and I can assure you, having seen the diamonds Yvonne has extracted from her protector, she has no intention of losing him."

"Well, you are a braver man than I am," Lord Rowlock remarked.

"What you need is more push and determination to get what you want in this world," the Duke said.

"You really believe that?" Lord Rowlock enquired in a different tone of voice.

"I have always got exactly what I wanted out of life," the Duke replied. "I have not only been determined, but have taken certain risks in attaining it."

He laughed.

"When I make love to Staverton's mistress in Staverton's bed, having drunk Staverton's excellent champagne, I congratulate myself on being extremely clever."

"I drink to that," Lord Rowlock said. "And I drink to you, Ranelagh. You have given me an idea, and if it comes off I shall thank you in all sincerity."

"I am delighted to be of assistance," the Duke replied.

Petrina heard their glasses clink as they must have touched across the supper-table.

She had eavesdropped because she could not help it, but now she felt angry that the Duke of Ranelagh and Lord Rowlock, whom she had been told to eliminate from her list of acquaintances, should be laughing at the Earl and thinking that they had scored off him.

She had however little time to consider what she had learnt, for the Viscount reappeared to tell them that Yvonne Vouvray would be singing at any moment.

He had hardly sat down in the alcove before a Master of Ceremonies, following a roll of drums, announced the Prima Donna from the balcony of the Rotunda.

"My Lords, Ladies and Gentlemen! Tonight we have the great honour and privilege to hear one of the most famous Prima Donnas in all Europe. A citizen of France, she has sung at the famous Opera House in Paris and at La Scala in Milan, and she is known as 'the Nightingale.'

"My Lords, Ladies and Gentlemen! I have the supreme pleasure to present for your delectation and delight *Mademoiselle* Yvonne Vouvray!"

There was a great burst of applause and the Master of Ceremonies drew to the front of the balcony the famous soprano.

Even at a distance from where she was sitting Petrina could see how attractive the Frenchwoman was.

She had dark hair, even darker than Lady Isolda's, and it seemed to glow with blue lights.

Her eyes were enormous, fringed with long eyelashes, and her lips were crimson. She was exquisitely dressed in a gown which shimmered with diamanté, which reflected the oil-lights so that she glittered as if she were clothed in moon-beams.

She began to sing and there was no doubt that she deserved all the praise that had been lavished upon her by the critics.

It was a compliment which all performers appreciate that everyone listening was still and completely silent.

Her voice had the rare, exquisitely clear quality of a young boy's and yet as she sang she looked very feminine and extremely seductive.

Her figure was slightly voluptuous, but her long neck and rounded arms were those of a young goddess.

As she listened, Petrina knew her voice had an allure that was irresistible, and looking at her she felt suddenly a sharp pain within herself that was so intense that it was physical as well as mental.

"She is lovely, attractive, no wonder he . . ."

She stopped because it was so painful to think that this exquisite creature, this woman with the voice that justified her being called "the Nightingale," should belong to the Earl.

For a moment she could not understand why the knowledge of it hurt her and why the pain in her heart seemed to intensify with every note that Yvonne Vouvray sang.

Then Petrina suddenly knew the truth, and the horror of it made her want to cry out a denial.

Yet it was impossible not to realise that she was jealous, jealous of the Earl's mistress, jealous with a pain and an agony that was like a sword thrusting into her flesh.

Jealous because she loved him!

Chapter Five

"I have made arrangements for us to dine at Devonshire House this evening," the Dowager Duchess said. "We are not wanted here, as my grandson is giving a dinner-party."

"A dinner-party?" Petrina asked, supposing it was to be for men only.

The Dowager Duchess smiled.

"The Prince Regent had invited himself," she said, "and although there will be a number of beautiful women present, the main topic of conversation will centre round another female."

Petrina looked at her questioningly and the Dowager Duchess went on:

"Durwin is determined to win the Gold Cup at Ascot with his horse Bella, while the Prince is quite certain that his entry will be the victor."

Petrina could understand that the conversation would be a very spirited one between the rival owners, and she was certain that other distinguished members of the Jockey Club would also be there. But she felt a trifle piqued that she was not to be present.

As if she knew what Petrina was thinking, the Dowager Duchess said:

"The Prince Regent likes older and more sophisticated women. He will of course be bringing Lady Hertford with him, and I am quite certain that Lady

Isolda has managed to get herself included one way or another."

There was a cold note in the Dowager Duchess's voice because, as Petrina knew, she disliked Lady Isolda, but no more than Petrina herself did.

Ever since she had admitted to herself that she was in love with the Earl and was jealous of the ladies on whom he bestowed his favours, she had felt every day was more agonising than the last.

She was not only continually tortured by the attractions of Yvonne Vouvray but by the beauty of Lady Isolda Herbert.

She had no idea, of course, that the Earl was finding Lady Isolda's persistent demands on him more and more irritating, or that there was an increasing number of scented effusions written in her flowing hand lying unopened in a drawer of his desk.

All that Petrina knew was that at every Ball, Reception, or Assembly they attended Lady Isolda gravitated to the Earl's side as if he were a magnet, and that day after day she saw grooms wearing the Herbert livery delivering notes at the front door.

'I am glad I am not going to be present at the dinner-party this evening,' she thought.

She knew it would be difficult to attend to the gentlemen seated on either side of her when she would be watching the Earl, knowing that Lady Isolda, doubtless beside him, would be holding his attention.

It was impossible to suppose that he was not infatuated by her outstanding beauty, and Petrina felt despairingly that it was only a question of time, perhaps only of days, before their engagement was announced.

"I love him!" she admitted to herself in the darkness of the night, and all through the day she found herself waiting and looking for his broad shoulders, his dark head, and his handsome, rather cynical face.

He had been exceedingly kind in taking her, as he had promised, to meet the Vicar of St. James's in Piccadilly.

There Petrina had listened to what the Clergy were trying to do for the unwanted children in their Parishes, who were abandoned sometimes inside the Church itself.

They were handicapped, as the Earl had said, by lack of funds, though at least they were making a small step in the right direction.

But Petrina felt that they were not trying hard enough to prevent the young girls who came from the country from being seduced into a life of sin before they realised what was happening to them.

"Would it not be possible," she asked, "to have someone like yourself, Vicar, or perhaps even a woman, on duty at the Inns where the stage-coaches disembark their passengers, so that if a young girl arrives looking helpless and bewildered, she could be taken to a place of safety or escorted to the house where she has been engaged as a servant?"

"It is certainly an idea, Miss Lyndon," the Vicar answered, "but quite frankly, I have not enough helpers to call upon and I doubt if the majority of young girls who come to London would listen to anyone speaking to them for their own good."

This, Petrina felt, was a defeatist attitude, and when she had left the Vicarage and was alone with the Earl she persisted in her idea, saying she was sure it was something that could be done.

"I will discuss it with the Police," the Earl said.

"A country girl might be frightened of a Policeman speaking to her," Petrina said. "What we want is an elderly woman, kind and maternal, who would gain their confidence and make them understand how careful they must be."

The Earl did not reply, but he knew there were quite a number of women such as Petrina had described waiting for girls who came off the stage-coaches.

They were procuresses, who with promises of good employment and high wages lured their victims away to houses of disrepute from which later there was no escape.

"I promise you I will go into the whole problem," the Earl said, "and I have already discussed the matter with Lord Ashley, who is one of our foremost Reformers. But you must not be impatient if we do not get results very quickly."

"I am impatient!" Petrina answered. "Every day, every hour that we are wasting time, more young girls are ruined, and more miserable, unwanted little babies are born into the world."

There was a passion in her voice which the Earl found very moving.

In all his acquaintance with the female sex he had never met anyone who had cared so deeply for what happened to less fortunate women than themselves.

He found himself looking with different eyes at the prostitutes he saw as he drove through the streets, and reading the newspaper reports on crime with more attention than he had done in the past.

A number of his friends were extremely surprised when he spoke seriously to them on the subject, quoting passages from the reports of the Select Committee.

"I should have thought, Staverton, you had enough women to worry about without including the poor Droxies," one Member of Parliament joked.

But the others paid attention to what he said, knowing that he had a powerful position in the House of Lords.

He had certainly been kind, Petrina thought, but that was not to say he was interested in her personally; and after all, why should he be when he already had two such seductive and alluring women of his own?

Because she was in love and because she could think of nothing but the Earl, she slept badly, and the Dowager Duchess noticed that she was thinner.

"I think it is a good thing that the Season will soon be at an end," she said. "These late nights with so much dancing will be taking their toll of your looks if we are not careful."

"The Season will be at an end!" Petrina repeated almost beneath her breath.

She wondered what she would do then and if the Earl had any plans for her. Because she could not bear to think he might send her away to the country, or even to Harrogate, she dared not ask questions.

But she had learnt that when Ascot was over the Prince Regent would go to Brighton. Then gradually all the great houses would be shut up and their owners would either follow His Royal Highness or retire to their country estates until the autumn.

Petrina asked Mr. Richardson who was dining at Staverton House that evening, and he showed her a list of the guests.

There were only twenty of them, headed of course by the Prince Regent and Lady Hertford, and Lady Isolda's name seemed to jump out of the paper and flash itself in front of Petrina's eyes.

She went out to dinner with the Dowager Duchess, feeling like Cinderella, who had not been invited to the Ball.

As there was only a small family dinner at Devonshire House, they returned early, and as they stepped out at the pillared entrance the Major Domo informed them:

"The ladies have only just retired to the Salon, Your Grace, and the gentlemen are still in the Dining-Room."

"Then we will slip upstairs without being seen," the Dowager Duchess said with a smile.

She kissed Petrina on her cheek, saying:

"Good-night, my dear. Do not wait for me. You know I have to take the stairs slowly."

"Good-night, Ma'am," Petrina replied, curtseying.

As the Dowager Duchess put her hand on the bannister and started to move slowly step by step up the stairway, Petrina said:

"There is a book I want to read in the Blue Drawing-Room. I will just go fetch it."

She knew she would encounter no-one in that room, for it was never used in the evening. She found the book she wanted and also a magazine which she had been reading earlier in the day.

She had picked them up and turned towards the door when she had a longing to go out into the air.

She knew it was unlikely that she would sleep once she was in her bed.

It had been very hot during the last two days, almost too hot to enjoy riding in the Park, and Petrina wanted to feel the coolness of the night on her cheeks.

She put down the books she had in her hand, drew back the heavy satin curtains, and opened a French window which led onto the terrace.

As she stepped outside she could hear voices coming from the Salon and also masculine laughter from the Dining-Room, whose windows also overlooked the garden.

Petrina, however, slipped down the flight of steps and walked over the lawn in the shadows.

It was, as she had expected, pleasantly cool, and when she was away from the lights of the house, the moon and stars in the sky above were brilliant enough for her to find the way without falling into the flower-beds or brushing against the shrubs.

She remembered there was a seat at the far end of the garden not far from the door in the wall which she and the Earl had used the night she had robbed Sir Mortimer's house.

She thought she would sit there and try not to think

of how beautiful Lady Isolda was or how alluring Yvonne Vouvray was. There were so many other things, she told herself, that should occupy her mind.

Because she was in love she wanted, as every other woman has done since the beginning of time, to be better, cleverer, and more beautiful for the man she loved.

The Earl was so clever, she thought, that it was obvious that he would find her ignorance on so many subjects boring.

Because she was modest about her own capabilities, Petrina was certain that Lady Isolda could discuss politics, racing, and every other interest he had with a knowledge which because she was so much younger she could not hope to emulate.

"But I will try," she told herself fiercely, "I will try!"

The book she was reading and which she had fetched to take up to bed with her concerned the history of thoroughbreds and the breeding of racehorses.

She had nearly reached the seat she was seeking, and as her eyes searched for its outline in the shadows she saw with astonishment someone rise from it and move quickly out of sight into the shrubs.

She stood still.

"Who is there?" she called.

There was no reply.

"I saw you," she said accusingly, "so there is no point in hiding!"

She thought it must be one of the servants and knew that they were not allowed in the garden.

She reached the seat and as the shrubs behind it were not very thick she thought she saw a figure standing in the midst of them.

"Come out," she ordered firmly. "Unless you want me to call for one of the footmen to make you do so."

The shrubs parted and from them there came a man.

She could see his face by the light from the sky and she realised he was a stranger and not, as she had expected, one of the household.

"Who are you?" she asked. "And why are you here?"

"I must apologise," he replied.

"You realise that you are trespassing?"

"Yes, and I will leave at once."

Petrina looked at him uncertainly, then she said:

"If you are a thief or a burglar, I should not allow you to do so."

"I promise you, Miss Lyndon, that I have no intention of stealing anything."

"You know who I am?" Petrina asked.

"Yes."

"But how, and why are you here?"

"I would rather not answer that question, but I promise you I will not do any material harm and I will leave at once if you wish."

"What do you mean by 'material harm'?" Petrina asked.

The stranger smiled and she realised he was young, under twenty-five, and although she could not see him clearly she knew he was dressed neatly, but not with the elegance that might be expected from a gentleman.

"Who are you?" she asked again.

"My name is Nicholas Thornton, which will mean nothing to you."

"What do you do?"

"I am a reporter."

"You are a reporter?" Petrina echoed, then added:

"You mean you are here to report on what is happening tonight? I am sure the Earl would not like that. This is a private party."

She knew that when the Prince dined privately with one of his friends, every step was taken to prevent it coming to the notice of the press.

Nicholas Thornton smiled again.

"I can promise you, Miss Lyndon, that His Royal Highness's presence at Staverton House is not my main reason for being here."

"Then what?" Petrina enquired.

"That is something I cannot tell you, but I would be grateful if you would allow me to stay."

"How did you get in, as a matter of interest?" she asked.

"I climbed over the wall."

"Then you most certainly are trespassing. If I were doing what is right, I should be screaming loudly for help and have you thrown out."

"I am aware of that, but because I know you are kind to people less fortunate than yourself, I beg you to let me stay."

"How do you know I am kind?" Petrina asked suspiciously.

"I have heard about the money you have been giving to the women on the streets."

"If you have heard about it, please do not write anything about it for your newspaper," Petrina said pleadingly. "It would annoy my Guardian exceedingly and I too would not wish it to become known publicly."

Nicholas Thornton did not answer and Petrina said:

"Please . . . I am asking you this as a favour."

"May I ask one in return?"

"What is it?"

"That you let me stay."

"I suppose that is reasonable," Petrina said doubtfully, "but I should like you to tell me why."

"I will tell you if you swear that you will not change your mind and have me thrown out of the garden."

"I can only decide that when I hear what you have to say," she answered.

She was trying to be cautious, at the same time, she was aware how much the Earl would dislike any publicity about her generosity to the prostitutes in Piccadilly and she knew how shocked the Dowager Duchess would be at the thought of her speaking to such women.

She sat down on the seat, feeling rather helpless.

"Tell me what you want," she said, "and I will try to understand."

"That is kind of you, Miss Lyndon," Nicholas Thornton said, seating himself beside her, "because although it may not seem of much consequence to you, it is extremely important to me personally."

"Why?"

"Because if I can get a story tonight it might affect my whole future."

"How could it do that?"

"Have you ever heard of someone called William Hone?"

"I do not think so," Petrina replied.

"He is what is commonly called a 'Press Hero,' " Nicholas Thornton explained. "He has been a Reformer since 1796, when at age sixteen he joined the London Correspondents Society."

"What does he do?" Petrina asked.

"He owns the *Weekly Reformists Register*."

"I have heard of that," Petrina said. "In fact I have read issues of it."

"I write for it," Nicholas Thornton told her, "but William Hone was in prison last year and because he was not there the paper almost faded away."

"What is he doing now?" Petrina asked.

"He is free, and he intends to bring out a newspaper called *John Bull*. He has promised me a good position on it if it goes well, and I think it will."

"But it is not yet published?"

"It takes time to bring out a new paper," Nicholas Thornton said. "In the meantime, I am trying to show William Hone exactly what stories I can produce, and he has arranged to have them published by a friend of his who owns the *Courier*."

"I understand," Petrina said, "but what is this story which is so important to you?"

"I am going to be quite honest with you, Miss Lyndon," Nicholas Thornton said, "because without your goodwill I shall be turned out of the garden. Then I shall be forced, of course, to use the story about you rather than the one I have come here to obtain."

He spoke pleasantly and quietly, but Petrina was well aware of the threat behind his words.

"Tell me," she said.

"You know Lady Isolda Herbert?" Nicholas Thornton questioned.

"Of course."

"And you know that everyone is expecting her engagement to the Earl of Staverton to be announced at any moment?"

"Yes," Petrina said in a low voice.

"Well, apparently," Nicholas Thornton went on, "the Earl is lagging his feet, and Her Ladyship is finding it difficult to make him say the words that will make her the Countess of Staverton."

Petrina did not speak. She only felt that the pain of what this man was saying stabbed at her as if he used a weapon.

"Lady Isolda has thought up a little scheme of her own," Nicholas Thornton continued.

Petrina stiffened to attention.

"A scheme of her own?" she repeated. "What is it?"

"She has asked me to wait here and note the exact time she leaves the party, which she insists will be several hours after the departure of the Prince Regent."

"What do you mean? What are you saying?" Petrina asked.

Even as she asked the question she saw all too clearly what Lady Isolda intended.

It would be quite understandable that a newspaper, if they knew of it, should report that the Prince Regent accompanied by Lady Hertford had dined at Staverton House.

It would also be of considerable interest to the gossip-loving *Beau Monde* if they learnt that Lady Isolda Herbert had stayed on afterwards and had not returned to her own house until the early hours of the following day.

There was no doubt of the construction that would be put upon the prolongation of her visit, and the Earl would be forced to make honourable amends for the damage to her reputation by offering her marriage.

Petrina had her suspicions as to where the Earl had been the night he had caught her climbing down the drain-pipe with the stolen letters.

She knew that Lady Isolda's house was only a short distance from his own, but while the Earl might walk home unnoticed, Her Ladyship would drive with all pomp and ceremony from the front door of Staverton House and her servants as well as the Earl's would be aware that what the newspapers reported was true.

The Earl's bed-room in the East Wing overlooked the garden, and perhaps, Petrina thought, Nicholas Thornton would be watching for the light in that window while the others in Staverton House were dark.

It was just the sort of idea that someone like Lady Isolda Herbert would think up, which she knew would force the Earl into marriage simply because it would be impossible for him to do other than the honourable thing.

Petrina had learnt since coming to London of some

of the unwritten but very stringent rules by which Society regimented its members.

A gentleman could drink himself under the table, own an astronomical amount of money, and have innumerable love-affairs with ladies and anyone else he fancied, but he must not offend the Social Code.

This protected a lady's reputation, and Petrina knew that the Earl, if he offended, would be forced by public opinion to make retribution.

It was a clever plan, but at the same time everything she felt for him cried out against it.

The Earl had told her with his own lips that he had no wish to marry Lady Isolda or anyone else, and she believed him. It was only jealousy that had made her suspect, during the last few days when Lady Isolda's groom was continually knocking on the door, that he was weakening in that resolve.

Now that she had learnt that he was being pressured into doing what he had no wish to do, she knew she must save him.

Her thoughts were turning over and over in her mind, but she had not spoken, and after some moments of silence Nicholas Thornton said a little anxiously:

"I hope you will help me."

His words seemed to come to Petrina out of a fog and she thought frantically that while she had to help him she must somehow prevent him from doing anything which would hurt the Earl.

"How much is Lady Isolda paying you?" she asked.

"Ten sovereigns," Nicholas Thornton answered.

"I will give you twenty," Petrina said quickly.

"It is kind of you, Miss Lyndon, and of course I accept," Nicholas Thornton replied, "but I still have to have a story. My whole future is at stake!"

"A story! A story!"

The two words seemed to repeat themselves over and over in Petrina's brain. Then slowly an idea

seemed to form itself piece by piece as if it were a
jig-saw puzzle and she said aloud:

"If I give you twenty pounds and a really good story,
will you promise not to mention the Earl in any way,
especially in connection with Lady Isolda?"

"A good story?" Nicholas Thornton questioned.

"A very good story," Petrina replied.

"Whom does it concern."

"The Duke of Ranelagh."

"He is news. Anything about him would certainly
be acceptable."

"Then listen to me . . ." Petrina said, lowering her
voice.

*　　*　　*

"Are we going to Ascot?" Petrina enquired of the
Dowager Duchess.

The Dowager Duchess shook her head.

"Not to stay. I hope you will not be disappointed,
dearest child, but I really could not attend the races
for three days without being completely exhausted."

"No, of course not," Petrina agreed.

"I thought we might drive down for the Gold Cup,"
the Dowager Duchess said, "to back Bella as Durwin
will expect us to do."

"That would be delightful," Petrina agreed.

But she could not prevent herself from asking:

"Will he drive with us?"

The Dowager Duchess shook her head.

"No, he is staying at Windsor Castle. The Prince
Regent likes to have him there and we are not included in the invitation."

The Dowager Duchess's voice was slightly spiteful
as she added:

"I would not really wish to have Lady Hertford patronising me and showing off that she is the hostess. I find it impossible to tolerate that woman!"

"Then it is a good thing we are staying in London," Petrina said with a smile.

"We have already been invited to luncheon in the Royal Box on Gold Cup day," the Dowager Duchess said. "You will find that amusing, and you will be able to wear that pretty gown you bought last week."

"That will be lovely!" Petrina enthused.

But as soon as she was alone she dashed off a note and told a footman to take it to an address which made him raise his eye-brows when he was out of her presence.

Two days later, when the Earl had left for Windsor Castle, driving his team of black horses and looking extremely dashing in a new Phaeton painted in the yellow and black of his family colours, Petrina received a reply to her letter.

She read it, concealed it in her reticule, then went to the Dowager Duchess's Sitting-Room.

"Have you anything particular planned for this evening, Ma'am?" she asked.

"We have no invitations," the Dowager Duchess replied. "As you know, everybody has either gone to Ascot or is pretending to have done so. Our next Ball is on Friday evening after the racing is over."

"Then if you do not mind, Ma'am, I would like to dine with Claire tonight."

"Yes, of course," the Dowager Duchess approved, "and it will give me a chance to have dinner in bed. My leg has been tiresome lately and the Doctor keeps telling me I must rest."

"Then you must be very quiet for the next two days," Petrina said, "and if you do not wish to go to Ascot on Thursday, I shall quite understand."

"And miss seeing Durwin's horse win the Gold Cup?" the Dowager Duchess cried. "Leg or no leg, I must be there to see Bella pass the Winning Post."

"Of course!" Petrina smiled. "In the meantime, rest as much as you can. You have been so kind in taking me everywhere, and I know at times you feel very tired."

"There is nothing more tiring or tiresome than old age," the Dowager Duchess replied, "but I can assure you I would not have missed your Season for anything in the world!"

Petrina kissed her, then went to her own room to make plans for the evening.

She naturally had to leave the house in one of the Earl's carriages, which deposited her at Claire's house.

She had already ascertained that Claire was at Ascot, staying with her future father-in-law, and when the Marquess of Morecombe's Butler looked at her in surprise, she said:

"I know Lady Claire is away, but I have a very important message for her to receive the moment she returns. Would you permit me to write it down?"

"Yes, of course, Miss," the Butler replied, and showed Petrina into the Morning-Room.

She scribbled down something which was not of the least importance, sealed it, and handed it to the Butler.

"I should be most grateful if you would see that Lady Claire has it in her hand the moment she returns from Ascot."

"You may leave it to me, Miss," the Butler answered.

He opened the door and looked out into the Square and was astonished to see the carriage disappearing.

"Oh, dear!" Petrina exclaimed in dismay. "The coachman could not have understood that I wanted him to wait. I expect he thought I was dining here as I do so often."

"There has obviously been a misunderstanding," the Butler said.

"Will you please call me a hackney carriage?"
Petrina asked.

There was nothing else the man could do, and
Petrina drove off, the coachman having been told to
take her to Staverton House.

As soon as they left the Square she gave him another address, and when she arrived at Paradise Row
in Chelsea it was to find Nicholas Thornton waiting
for her.

She stepped out, gave him the money to pay the
coachman, and asked:

"You have got them?"

"I have them here," he said, holding out a parcel.

"That is good," Petrina said, "and here is the money
I promised you."

She handed him an envelope as she spoke and Nicholas Thornton pushed it into his pocket.

"Is everything arranged?" she asked.

"Everything we planned," he answered. "That is the
house."

He pointed to the one on the corner, which Petrina
realised was very attractive.

It had an elegant front door with a fan-light above
it, carved porticos, and corniced eaves with deep
sashed windows.

The houses in Paradise Row had, she had learnt
since she first heard the name, been built during the
Stuart times, and one of its first occupants was the
beautiful, warm-hearted, and feckless Duchess de
Mazarin, who had captured the heart of Charles II.

The King had made her an allowance of four thousand pounds a year. Her principal fault, Petrina had
learnt in the books she studied, had been an obsession
with gambling, and after the King's death when her
debts had become a serious embarrassment she retired
permanently to the house in Paradise Row.

'The King's mistress and the Earl's mistress!'
Petrina thought to herself.

Then she put everything from her mind to listen to
what Nicholas Thornton was telling her.

"If we move a little way down the Row," he said,
"there is an empty house where we can sit on the
door-step while we wait."

"It will certainly be more comfortable," Petrina answered.

She let him lead her to the front of the empty house
and from there, where no-one entering was likely to
notice them, they could see the front door that belonged to Yvonne Vouvray.

Nicholas Thornton dusted the stone step with his
handkerchief and Petrina sat down.

She had a feeling that she was doing something extremely reprehensible. At the same time, it was the
only way she could think of to save the Earl from Lady
Isolda; and she had to keep her side of the bargain
with Nicholas Thornton.

She had just seated herself when he said:

"Wait a minute, we might as well be comfortable.
I brought some hay here earlier in the day."

Petrina looked to see a bundle of hay pressed into
the shadows of the front door where it was not likely
to be noticed.

Nicholas Thornton brought it out and heaped some
of it on the top step to make a soft seat for Petrina.

She laughed as she said:

"It is as good as a cushion any day!"

When she had once again seated herself he brought a
package out of his pocket and handed it to her.

"What is this?" she asked.

"Something to eat," he answered. "I knew you
would go without your dinner and I thought you might
be hungry."

"You think of everything," Petrina said.

"Detail in a campaign is always important," he said solemnly, and they both laughed.

She opened the packet and found crusts of new bread and slices of ham and cheese, which they shared.

"How long do you think we will have to wait?" Petrina asked after they had munched for a little while in silence.

"Not as long as we had expected."

"Why not?"

"Because I heard today that *Mademoiselle* Yvonne is not singing at Vauxhall tonight."

"Not singing at Vauxhall?"

"No. She is at home, resting. They told me so at the Gardens."

"But why?"

"Well, from the tradesmen I have noticed calling at the house today, I think she is entertaining someone important for dinner."

"You really think so? Surely that is rather a risk?"

"Who is likely to know? The Earl is at Ascot, and if she takes a night off because she is feeling unwell, Vauxhall Gardens will find another entertainer and no-one will worry what she is really doing one way or another."

"No, of course not," Petrina agreed. "What is the time now?"

"My watch is in pawn," Nicholas Thornton replied, "but I should imagine it must be after eight o'clock."

"Yes, I am sure it is," Petrina said. "I left Staverton House just before seven-thirty because the Morecombes usually dine rather early."

"I see that you think of detail, too," Nicholas Thornton said with a smile.

"Did you remember the boys?" Petrina asked hastily, as if she had just thought of them.

"Of course," he answered. "Do not worry, everything is going well so far."

Petrina drew her breath and crossed her fingers.

"Do not boast," she begged.

"I am not," he answered, "and I am in fact much more anxious than you are."

"The difference is that you do not show it," Petrina replied.

He did not answer, but sat clasping his knees, watching the house on the corner.

He had a thin, rather sensitive face and there was something about him which told Petrina she could trust him.

She was sure that he was intelligent and that he wrote well. It was, however, a pity that he had to stoop to mere vulgar gossip which sold the papers that attacked the Regent and the Government.

But she had a feeling that he was capable of writing much more intelligent articles and she was determined to talk to him about the reforms of which such newspapers as the *Courier* and certainly *John Bull* would be in favour.

But this, she felt, was not the moment, and it was difficult to have thoughts beyond anything but the plan they had worked out between them.

Then almost as if in answer to their prayers a closed carriage came down the street and drew up outside the house on the corner.

"The Duke!" Petrina whispered as it passed, for she had recognised the painted coat-of-arms on the door.

Nicholas Thornton nodded and they both watched the footman get down from the box to raise the knocker before he opened the door of the carriage.

The Duke stepped out and Petrina thought that he entered the house hurriedly. Then the door shut behind him and the carriage drove away.

She felt a sudden surge of anger, not against the Duke but against the woman to whom the Earl had given so much and who was deceiving him blatantly with another man.

"How can she do this?" Petrina asked herself, knowing that she personally had not been very impressed with the Duke.

Then she remembered her father saying once:

"The English are snobs—every one of them from the Prince to the poorest of his subjects. They are exceeded only by the French, who are the biggest snobs in the whole of Europe."

'I suppose a Duke means more than an Earl,' Petrina thought.

She knew that even if the Earl were of no importance whatsoever she would still love him, still feel that he was a King among men.

"Now, we have to wait until it is dark," Nicholas Thornton said at her side.

That, Petrina knew, was not going to be for some hours, and she helped herself to another slice of ham.

Actually the hours did not seem as long as she had anticipated, because, despite her resolution to the contrary, she could not help talking to Nicholas Thornton of the state of the country.

That inevitably led to the state of London and the women she was trying to help.

She learnt from him that there were not only boys in the Flash Houses but also girls.

"There are up to four hundred in St. Giles's, alone," Nicholas said. "I have been there, and it's the nearest thing to hell on earth that I have ever seen."

He told her how shocked and appalled he had been when he first came to London.

The son of a Solicitor in a small market town, he had always wanted to write and had refused, to his father's annoyance, to join the family firm.

He had come to London determined to make his own way in the world, and he had drifted from one newspaper to another until he met William Hone and realised that with him he would have an opportunity to write as he wished to do.

He told Petrina how the Prince Regent and quite a number of other people paid suppression money to the newspapers not to publish unpleasant things about them.

The Prince Regent paid particularly to suppress lampoons and caricatures.

George Cruikshank, one of the greatest known cartoonists, had received, Petrina learnt, one hundred pounds for a pledge not to caricature the Prince in any immoral situation, and publishers found that it paid them to be always angling for suppression money.

"It seems wrong that things that should be said should be suppressed," Petrina said.

"I agree with you," Nicholas Thornton answered, "and one day I will own a newspaper of my own. I swear to you I will then print the truth, come hell or high water!"

Petrina laughed.

"I will help you," she said, "and that is a promise."

They smiled at each other and started on the subject of corruption, which carried them through the next two hours.

At last it began to get dark and now the light they had been waiting for appeared in a first-floor window of the house on the corner.

Nicholas Thornton had got a general plan of the house and Petrina was certain he was right when he showed her which was the bed-room that Yvonne Vouvray occupied.

Half an hour passed. Now there were only two gas-lamps in the distance outside the Royal Hospital to shine through the darkness and the moon rising in the sky.

There was the sound of footsteps and two ragged boys of about ten years old appeared.

Nicholas Thornton greeted them by name.

"Now you know what to do, Bill," he said to the taller of the two. "Hurry off to the Hand-in-Hand Fire

Brigade and tell them they are wanted at once in
Paradise Row. Tell them to hurry, as the house belongs to the Earl of Staverton, who has paid his sub-
scription."

"Oi understand, Sir," Bill answered.

"We will give you ten minutes to get there," Nicholas Thornton said, "then come back and you will get
your money."

"Oi'll be back right enough, Sir," Bill answered
and hurried off up the street.

Nicholas Thornton handed the other boy what was
left of the bale of hay.

"Throw it over the railings into the basement, Sam,"
he said, "but do not spread it too thin."

Sam crossed the road and they watched him doing
what he had been told, then he returned to scrape up
the hay on which Petrina had been sitting and added it
to the rest.

In the meantime, Nicholas Thornton had been
opening the parcel which he had carried with him,
and Petrina saw that he had brought a number of
different fireworks, all of the sort which take longer to
burn than those which like rockets sweep up into the
sky.

Fireworks were very popular in the Pleasure Gardens of London and Vauxhall staged displays almost
every week.

Petrina, when she was at School, had read of the
great display that had been given in London when
the peace was announced four years ago, and she
knew that the Anniversary of the Battle of the Nile
was celebrated every year with fireworks.

They had always excited her ever since she was a
child, and she thought that now for the first time in
her life they were really serving a purpose. With the
assorted collection that Nicholas Thornton had
brought, it was difficult to see how their plan could not
be successful.

They sat waiting and now for the first time Nicholas Thornton seemed nervous.

He tapped with his fingers on his knee, then on the stone step on which he was sitting. Finally he collected the fireworks together.

"Bill should have alerted the Fire Brigade by now," he said.

He crossed the road, carrying the fireworks with him, and it was difficult for Petrina, who remained on the door-step, to see what he was doing.

Then there was the first glimmer of light from the firework he held in his hands before he threw it into the hay in the basement.

Immediately she could see a red glow against the walls of the house, then as Nicholas threw the other fireworks down to join the first there was a sudden explosion.

Now the hay was ignited and the flames combined with the sparks from the fireworks began to shoot up the side of the house.

Nicholas Thornton ran back across the road to stand beside Petrina.

She did not say anything, but only stood watching. Then, as he had been instructed, Sam ran along the road until he was standing outside the front of the house at the corner, where he started to shout: "Fire! Fire!" at the top of his voice.

A moment later the bed-room window opened and Petrina saw, by the light of the flames, the Duke put his head out.

He withdrew quickly and as he did so the fire-engine, drawn by two horses with six men riding on the traverse benches on either side of it, came round the corner, with its bell ringing.

The improved engine had the leather hose which had recently been invented and the very latest steel fire-escape ladder, and was equipped with the Captain

Manby portable extinguisher, which had come into use in 1816.

The Firemen, often called the Fire Police, had the uniform of the Hand-in-Hand Brigade, which Petrina had seen before and thought very impressive.

They wore red plush breeches with cotton stockings and silver-buckled shoes. Their jackets were of blue cloth with large silver buttons and on their heads they wore black, high-crowned hats.

The Hand-in-Hand had the famous mark of clasped hands surmounted by a crown, which had been theirs since 1679, and they were known to be the most reliable and most efficient Fire Brigade in the whole city.

The started work as soon as they appeared, hammering on the door and ordering the occupants of the house to evacuate it immediately.

They were obeyed so quickly that Petrina was certain the Duke and Yvonne Vouvray must already have been in the Hall, ready to leave.

They came out onto the pavement, the Duke wearing his pantaloons but obviously naked above the waist with the exception of a green silk bed-spread which he wore round his shoulders.

Yvonne Vouvray, on the other hand, wore an elaborate and very attractive negligé of rose-pink satin trimmed with lace and ribbons.

Her dark hair was falling over her shoulders, and even though she appeared agitated and frightened she looked, Petrina jealously admitted, extremely attractive.

They crossed over to the other side of the roadway to be out of the way of the Firemen who were pouring water through the leather hose onto the fire in the basement.

The fire was subsiding rapidly, and it was quite obvious that it had no hold on the house, as Nicholas Thornton with a note-book in his hand walked along the pavement to the watching couple.

"Has You Grace anything to say on this matter?" Petrina head him ask.

"Nothing!" the Duke replied sharply. "And I have no idea why you address me as 'Your Grace.'"

"I believe you to be the Duke of Ranelagh, Your Grace," Nicholas said.

"Quite untrue, and I forbid you to print such a libel."

"The public will be extremely interested in anything that concerns the famous *Mademoiselle* Yvonne Vouvray."

"I not wish *cette histoire* to be published," Yvonne Vouvray interposed. "Go away! *Allez!* Leave us alone! We not want reports in ze newspapers."

"I quite understand," Nicholas Thornton said.

He bowed, and would have walked away, but the Duke put out his hand to stop him.

"Look here, my man."

He spoke in a low voice, but Petrina was quite sure of what he was saying.

He was offering Nicholas Thornton a bribe, unaware, of course, that he had been bribed already and she had been wise enough to expect that this might happen.

"Whatever the Duke offers you to keep silent," she had said to Nicholas when they were making their plans, "I will give you more. I would not wish you to lose money because you are helping me."

"I am also helping myself," he said.

"But you are hard-up and you have been very kind," she answered.

She thought as she spoke that she would gladly give her whole fortune to save the Earl from having to marry Lady Isolda.

As she watched Nicholas coming back towards her, she decided she had killed two birds with one stone! In actual fact she had saved the Earl from two women, both of whom she hated.

Chapter Six

"I have brought back the brooch and bracelet I wore last night, Mr. Richardson," Petrina said, "and I wonder if I could choose some jewels for this evening?"

"Of course, Miss Lyndon," Mr. Richardson replied. "Were you thinking of a necklace or a brooch?"

"I think a necklace," Petrina answered. "I have a turquoise silk gown, and I think a turquoise necklace would look very nice with it."

"I am sure it would," Mr. Richardson replied.

He unlocked the safe and produced from it a number of leather-covered boxes which contained a dozen different necklaces.

The jewellery of the Staverton collection was so extensive that there were sets of almost every known jewel—diamonds, rubies, emeralds, sapphires, turquoises, and topaz. Petrina felt that each one she wore was more becoming than the last.

There were in fact three turquoise necklaces, one with the stones surrounded by diamonds, one by pearls, and a rather intriguing one set with both rubies and sapphires.

She was trying to decide which would look best with her gown, when the door of the Secretary's office opened and she heard a servant say:

"I've brought the keys of Paradise Row, Sir."

"Thank you, Clements," Mr. Richardson replied, "hang them on the board."

There was a board on one wall on which were hooked all the keys of the house and, Petrina imagined, all the other houses which were owned by the Earl.

She could not help giving a secret smile of satisfaction in assuming that Yvonne Vouvray had now vacated the house in Paradise Row and the Earl was free of her.

The story of the fire had received publicity first exclusively in the *Courier,* then was copied in a number of other newspapers.

There was also, Petrina learnt, a cartoon already on sale showing the Duke and Yvonne outside the house with the Firemen putting out the flames.

It had given spice to the story when it was learnt that the fire was nothing more serious than a blaze caused by fireworks.

The conflagration was therefore attributed either to . a practical joker or to the mischievous act of some small boys.

Whatever the explanation, it gave rise to a great deal of public interest, and although Petrina had no way of knowing what the Earl thought about it, she was quite certain that his reaction to the publicity would be to withdraw his protection from Yvonne Vouvray.

Her scheme had worked out according to plan and she was pleased.

When she went upstairs to change into her riding habit, she wondered if Lady Isolda had been disposed of so easily.

The Dowager Duchess was not feeling well and Petrina went to her room to tell her she was going riding in the Park accompanied by a groom.

"You look happy, my dear child," the Dowager

Duchess said perceptively, looking at Petrina's smiling face.

"It is a lovely day, Ma'am, and I only wish you were feeling better."

"I will try to get up for luncheon," the Dowager Duchess replied, "but if it is too much effort you must forgive me."

"If it is, I will have luncheon with you up here," Petrina promised.

"You must find out what Durwin is doing," the Dowager Duchess replied, then added with an exclamation: "But of course! I had forgotten! He told me he was driving to Chiswick to a prize-fight which is taking place this afternoon at Osterley Park."

"Then we will certainly have luncheon alone," Petrina answered.

She left the Dowager Duchess's bed-room and hurried down the stairs.

Her horse, which was a spirited bay, was waiting for her outside the front door.

As she came out onto the steps she saw that the Earl's black and yellow curricle was also waiting.

It was drawn by the black team which Petrina admired more every time she saw them, and she went to pat their noses, knowing that it would be hard to find a comparable quartet in the length and breadth of the country.

"I forgot to ask you," the Earl's voice said behind her. "How are you progressing with your driving?"

She had not heard him approach and she turned her head to find him standing beside her.

He looked as usual exceedingly magnificent, so that she felt as if her heart did a double-somersault at the sight of him.

"Abby is very pleased with me," she said, "and you told me yourself there are few drivers to compare with him."

"If Abby is satisfied," the Earl said, speaking of his Head-coachman, "then you must be very good. I presume one day you will wish to try your hand with these horses?"

Petrina's eyes lit up.

"Could I?" she asked. "It would be the most exciting present you could give me."

"Then we must make a date for you to take me driving," the Earl said, smiling.

Her eyes were shining like stars and she thought he looked at her in a kinder manner than she had ever known him to do before.

Then, at that moment, they were interrupted.

"Excuse me," a voice said, "but be ye Miss Lyndon?"

Both Petrina and the Earl turned to see an elderly man standing beside them.

He looked like a respectable shop-keeper and Petrina answered:

"Yes, I am Miss Lyndon."

"Pardon me for abothering ye, Miss," the man said, "but the' gentleman gave your name as guarantor for these purchases. Being in a small way of business, as ye might say, I can't afford outstanding accounts."

"What is it for?" Petrina asked, wondering what he could be speaking about.

"Fireworks, Miss."

Petrina drew in her breath.

"Fireworks?" she heard the Earl say in a questioning tone beside her. "Who purchased them?"

"T'were the beginning o' last week, Sir," the shop-keeper replied, "and they were bought by a Mr. Thornton, but as he had no money with him he gives me Miss Lyndon's name as guarantor. As he says she were astaying at Staverton House, I thinks I were safe in allowing him to take th' fireworks away with him."

"And what was the date?" the Earl asked.

There was something ominous in his tone which made Petrina feel as if she were watching herself fall over a cliff to destruction, and yet she could do nothing about it.

"T'were the sixth of June, Sir," the shop-keeper replied.

The Earl took the account from the man's hand and drew two sovereigns from his waist-coat pocket.

He handed them to the shop-keeper, who was immediately profuse in his thanks, but without waiting to hear what he had to say the Earl turned towards the house, giving Petrina one fleeting glance.

She knew, without his having to say so, that he expected her to follow him, and she walked behind him across the Hall, feeling as if she were on her way to the scaffold.

A footman opened the door of the Library and as Petrina entered she heard the door close behind her.

The Earl put the account down on his desk to stand for a moment looking at it.

Petrina's heart was beating so violently that she felt he must have heard it in the perceptible pause before he said abruptly:

"I want an explanation!"

Petrina drew in her breath.

"It was . . . to save . . . you," she said in a voice that was almost inaudible.

"To save me?" the Earl enquired. "What do you mean by that?"

"Lady Isolda had . . . paid a newspaper reporter to write something . . . unpleasant about you."

The Earl looked at her in genuine astonishment.

"What are you saying?" he enquired. "It is entirely incomprehensible to me."

"It . . . is true," Petrina said miserably. "I found Mr. Nicholas Thornton in the garden on the night the Prince Regent dined here."

"Nicholas Thornton? Who is this man?"

"A reporter on the *Courier*."

"You say he was in the garden? Why did you not call the servants to have him thrown out?"

"Because he told me that Lady Isolda had paid him ten sovereigns to report the ... time she left Staverton House ... which she ... intended to be ... a long time after your ... other guests had ... left."

"Can you be telling me the truth?" the Earl enquired.

"Why should I lie?" Petrina asked.

"Why should you be interested in what this man had been paid to write?"

There was a little pause before Petrina said:

"Lady Isolda believed it would ... force you into ... offering marriage to her ... and ... that is what he ... thought too."

The Earl gave an exclamation which sounded like a muffled oath. Then he said, and his voice was scathing:

"Why did you and this man need fireworks to use in a very different locality?"

"I ... I paid him double what Lady Isolda was ... giving him," Petrina stammered, "because he wanted a ... story. In fact he ... intended to have ... one."

The Earl looked down at the bill for the fireworks as if he could hardly believe his eyes, then he said slowly:

"Then you knew that the Duke of Ranelagh would be with *Mademoiselle* Vouvray. How could you have known such a thing?"

There was an uncomfortable silence before at last Petrina said in a very low voice:

"I ... overheard something the Duke said at ... V-Vauxhall Gardens."

"Vauxhall Gardens?"

The Earl almost shouted the words.

"When were you at Vauxhall Gardens?"

"C-Claire . . . took me one . . . night."

"Why?"

The question was like a pistol-shot, and somehow there was nothing Petrina could do but tell the truth.

"She knew I wanted to . . . hear *Mademoiselle* V-Vouvray."

"So you were aware she had some connection with me?"

"Y-yes."

The Earl's lips tightened and Petrina knew that he was seeing quite clearly what had happened.

Knowing where the Duke would be the night the Earl was at Windsor Castle, she had with Nicholas Thornton concocted the whole plot which would make, as she had promised him, "a good story."

There was a long silence and again Petrina was conscious of the beating of her heart and the fact that her lips were dry.

Then suddenly, so suddenly that she jumped, the Earl brought his fist down with all his force on the desk.

"Dammit!" he said. "It is inconceivable that I should be subjected to your curiosity and your interference in my private life!"

He looked at Petrina and his eyes were black with anger.

"How dare you behave in this manner!" he stormed. "How dare you intrigue with some common reporter."

"I . . . I did it to . . . save you."

"When I want you to save me, when I want your help in any way, I will ask for it!" the Earl almost shouted. "In the meantime, keep out of my life and my private affairs."

Petrina did not speak and after a moment he went on:

"It is intolerable, absolutely intolerable, that I should have to submit to this sort of behaviour from a young woman living under my roof, who should have

the decency and the modesty not even to think of a
world into which she should never intrude."

His voice rose and it was obvious that he had lost
his temper as he went on:

"Ever since I have known you, you have had an un-
healthy and unpleasant preoccupation with subjects
which are no concern of yours and would be distaste-
ful to anyone with the least sensibility."

He paused to add forcefully:

"All I can say is that I am appalled by your behaviour and I assure you I shall take stringent steps
immediately to see that I am not again subjected to
your impertinence."

His voice seemed to reverberate round the room.
Then in little more than a whisper Petrina said:

"I am . . . sorry if I made you . . . angry."

"Angry?" the Earl echoed. "I am not merely angry, I am disgusted! Get out of my sight."

He spoke so violently that Petrina gave a little cry
and turning ran from the room.

She pulled open the door, sped across the Hall, and
ran down the steps to where the horse and groom were
waiting for her.

She was helped into the saddle, then rode down the
drive, across Park Lane, and into Hyde Park.

She had no idea where she was going, she just
wanted to escape from the Earl's anger and the fury
in his voice, which made her feel as if he had struck
her.

She turned her horse's head towards the unfashion-
able part of the Park and rode looking straight ahead of
her, unaware even that the groom was following her.

She felt as if her whole world had collapsed about
her ears and there was nothing but ruin.

As she rode on, she told herself that the Earl had
been unjust and unfair.

He had not taken into consideration that everything

she had done had been for his sake, to save him from having to marry Lady Isolda and from being cheated by his mistress.

"He should really be grateful to me," Petrina told herself.

Now her own temper asserted itself and she no longer felt crushed and humiliated, but defiant.

She could understand the Earl being annoyed that she had, as he said, intrigued with Nicholas Thornton.

The consequences if she had not done so must be very obvious to him.

But the way he had spoken to her made her feel extremely resentful. As she rode over the bridge of the Serpentine towards Rotten Row, she told herself that he was definitely both unjust and ungrateful.

Petrina was deep in her thoughts and it therefore made her start when she heard a voice beside her saying:

"You are looking very serious, lovely Miss Lyndon. Am I still in your bad graces?"

Petrina turned her head to find that Lord Rowlock was riding beside her.

He swept his tall hat from his head as he spoke, looking so handsome as he did so that she felt that here was the chance to show what she thought of the Earl's behaviour.

"Good-morning, Lord Rowlock!" she said sweetly.

"You have been very cruel to me," he said, "but I hope that for whatever crime I have committed, I am now forgiven."

"It is not exactly a . . . crime," Petrina replied, feeling a little embarrassed. "It is just that my Guardian . . ."

"I understand," he interposed quickly. "Of course I understand. I know that the Earl told you I am a fortune-hunter, but what I feel for you, Petrina, is something very different."

Petrina knew she ought to ride away and prevent

Lord Rowlock from talking in such an intimate manner, and yet because she was smarting under a sense of injustice she found it impossible not to listen.

"I know all the things that are said against me," Lord Rowlock said in a low voice, "but I would have fallen in love with you, Petrina, if you had not had a penny in the world. God, do you realise how beautiful you are?"

There was a note of sincerity in his voice which Petrina, almost despite herself, found very moving.

"I am sorry," she said softly.

"You have made me very miserable!"

"There is nothing I can do about it."

"There is something you could do for me, if you would."

"What is that?" she asked nervously.

"You know I have very little money," Lord Rowlock said. "I have made no bones about that, but I made a bet the other night—and I suppose it was a very stupid one—that I would find a woman who could race a curricle with two horses against Lady Lawley, and win!"

"Race against Lady Lawley?" Petrina asked.

She knew that the lady in question was one of the most noted Whips in the *Beau Monde*.

It was fashionable for the more affluent Beaux to supply their mistresses with curricles and even Phaetons which they could drive themselves.

They either had their protector or a groom in attendance and the majority were capable only of driving up and down the Row to flaunt their clothes and their jewels before the less fortunate members of their profession.

In consequence, few ladies drove in public, but Lady Lawley was noted as being outstanding in handling her horses.

Petrina looked at Lord Rowlock with surprised eyes.

"Are you suggesting," she asked after a moment, "that I should drive against Lady Lawley?"

"Why not?" he questioned. "I have seen you driving in the Park and I thought how exceptionally well you handled the reins. Quite a number of my friends have said the same thing."

It was a compliment such as Petrina had never imagined receiving.

As she had told the Earl this morning, Abby was pleased with her and made her feel as if she personally had won the Gold Cup at Ascot.

That Lord Rowlock should consider she had a chance against Lady Lawley was more flattering than if he had compared her to the goddess Aphrodite or to the *Venus di Milo*.

"I might . . . let you . . . down," she said after a moment.

"I believe you could beat her," Lord Rowlock insisted. "She has been boasting that there is no woman except herself in the whole *Beau Monde* who has any idea of handling horse-flesh."

"That sounds very conceited," Petrina said.

"I want you to prove her wrong," Lord Rowlock said.

It was tempting, too tempting for Petrina to refuse.

"When is the race?" she asked.

"Anytime you wish," Lord Rowlock replied. "To-day, if you say the word."

Petrina recalled swiftly that the Earl would not be returning until late.

'He will not know,' she thought.

She would not feel so crushed and humiliated by him if she won the race against Lady Lawley.

"What time do we start and where?" she asked Lord Rowlock.

"I knew you would not fail me," he cried. "Could any woman be so sporting or so brave?"

Petrina found it impossible not to respond to the admiration in his eyes.

"I only hope I will not fail you."

"You could never do that," he answered, and she knew he was speaking not only of the race.

He arranged that he would collect her from Staverton House at one o'clock.

Petrina rode home hoping that the Dowager Duchess would decide not to rise for luncheon.

She found on her return that her wish had been granted, for the Dowager Duchess had left a message to say that she hoped she would excuse her but she was in such pain that she had taken a sleeping-tablet and did not wish to be disturbed.

Nothing could have worked out better, Petrina thought, as she went upstairs to change her clothes.

She put on a very elegant gown, one of her prettiest, feeling as she did so that she was defying the Earl not only in driving with Lord Rowlock but also by looking attractive.

The bonnet which matched her gown was not large enough to blow away in the wind and the ribbons which tied under her chin kept her hair neat and tidy beneath it.

She knew she was looking her best when, having eaten a light meal, she went into the Hall to await the arrival of His Lordship.

He drove up to the dront door in a curricle that was drawn by two well-matched chestnuts which, if not the equal of the Earl's superlative animals, were nevertheless well-bred and spirited.

Petrina's eyes were sparkling as Lord Rowlock helped her into the driving seat and she took the reins in her hands. She knew that she could handle the horses and was not in the least afraid of them.

They drove away from Staverton House and into the Park.

"Where do we meet Lady Lawley?" she asked.

"She is leaving at exactly the same time as we are," Lord Rowlock said, drawing a watch from his waist-coat pocket, "which is five minutes past one."

"Where from?"

"From Portman Square," he replied, "while we are leaving from Tyburn. We are on our honour not to leave a second before each other."

"Why from different places?" Petrina asked.

"Because the race is to all intents and purposes a test not only of horsemanship but also of ingenuity," he explained. "The first curricle to reach the Plume of Feathers, an Inn just off the Great North Road, is the winner, but there are no restrictions as to what route is followed."

He smiled at Petrina as he said:

"I have worked out an extremely ingenious way, which I think will defeat Lady Lawley from the on-set."

Petrina gave a little sigh.

It was a relief to know that the race did not depend only upon her.

While dressing she had thought of Lady Lawley's reputation as a Whip and had been afraid that however well she drove she could not equal a woman who was at least fifteen years older than she was and had a vast experience of driving.

She was quite prepared to believe that if the stakes were high Lord Rowlock would make every effort to be the winner, and when a moment later he said: "We can start!" she felt an irresistible excitement at the thought of the contest.

They drove off, Lord Rowlock directing her in a manner which told Petrina he knew all the different ways out of London.

He was clever enough, she noticed, to take her down quiet residential streets that were not filled with traffic, and soon they were free of the houses and moving out into the countryside.

It was a hot day, but there was a faint wind to relieve the heat. Petrina could soon give her horses their heads and feel the wind whip little tendrils of her hair round her flushed cheeks.

"This is exciting!" she said to Lord Rowlock. "I wonder if Her Ladyship is far ahead of us?"

"I am hoping she does not know the North of London as well as I do," he answered. "In fact, as the Lawleys have a house in Sussex, I think I was lucky in winning the toss."

"Is that how you decided which way we would go?" Petrina asked.

He nodded.

"The whole thing has been exceedingly fair," he explained, "and because I chose to go North I agreed to the slight handicap of our starting in the Park while Her Ladyship was a few streets nearer our goal."

Petrina looked serious.

"That means she could be well ahead of us."

"It is a possibility," he answered, "but I do not think you need worry."

"I am not going to," she answered, "and I like your horses."

"I wish they were mine," he said wistfully. "Actually they belong to a friend who lent them to me."

Petrina had a sudden suspicion that the friend was the Duke of Ranelagh, but she had no intention of asking too many questions.

She had no wish for Lord Rowlock to know she had been at Vauxhall Gardens the night she had overheard him and the Duke talking together.

They drove on and after an hour Petrina was looking anxiously ahead for a glimpse of Lady Lawley.

Although they passed a great number of curricles

they were all driven by gentlemen and there was no sign of Her Ladyship.

An hour later, when Petrina learnt that they were getting nearer to their objective, she asked:

"Supposing that when we get to the Plume of Feathers we find Lady Lawley already there—will you have lost a great deal of money?"

"More than I can afford," Lord Rowlock replied.

"How worrying," Petrina murmured.

"No-one could drive better than you are doing," he said, "and I do not need to tell you how grateful I am for your help and understanding."

"You can say that when we have won," Petrina answered, "but I cannot help feeling that Lady Lawley is ahead."

"She may quite easily be behind," Lord Rowlock said, and smiled.

"It is a fifty-fifty chance either way," Petrina replied.

Because she was so anxious to help him by winning, she whipped up the horses, and for the next half an hour they travelled faster than she had ever driven before.

'I do not believe the Earl himself could go faster driving a pair,' she thought.

The thought of the Earl brought an ache to her heart that she could not deny.

She tried not to think of him raging at her, the darkness of his eyes, the things he had said.

She thought at first that she had been almost numbed by the violence with which he had attacked her.

It had made her ready to defy him, but now she wished miserably that she had been able to explain how she had really tried to do what was best for him and had not thought of anything but saving him from having to marry Lady Isolda.

But she had the feeling that whatever she had said he would not have listened to her.

"You are looking worried," Lord Rowlock said beside her. "Let me tell you, Petrina, that if I do lose, it will be worth every penny to have had this opportunity of being with you and talking to you again."

"The Earl would be very annoyed if he knew where I was," Petrina said.

"He will never know," Lord Rowlock answered, "so do not worry about him."

Petrina remembered that they had to return to London and they had already been travelling for two and a half hours.

"Are we nearly there?" she asked anxiously.

"Only about two more miles," Lord Rowlock answered, and she felt relieved.

Petrina drew up at the Plume of Feathers, which was a delightful old Inn about half a mile off the main road.

It had a large yard and when she drove the curricle into it she saw with a sudden excitement that it was empty.

She pulled the horses to a standstill and turned to look at Lord Rowlock with sparkling eyes.

"We are first!" she exclaimed.

"I believe we are," he said.

He got out of the curricle and as the ostlers ran to the heads of the horses he asked:

"Has a curricle arrived driven by a lady?"

"No, Sir."

"We have done it!" Petrina cried. "We have done it! Oh, I am so glad, so happy for you!"

"I am more grateful than I can ever say," Lord Rowlock replied.

He took her hand in his and kissed it, then helped her from the curricle.

He gave instructions to the ostlers to stable the horses, rub them down, and water them, then he and Petrina walked into the Inn.

It was low-ceilinged and very attractive, with great

beams across the ceiling made from ships' timbers, and the Proprietor, obviously impressed by their appearance, hurried forward bowing to attend to them.

Petrina was taken upstairs by a mob-capped maid to a comfortable room with a big four-poster bed and a bow-window which overlooked the garden.

Petrina felt that anyone who stayed at the Plume of Feathers would be extremely comfortable.

She took off her bonnet, washed her hands, tidied her hair, then went downstairs to find Lord Rowlock waiting for her in a small private Parlour with an open bottle of champagne with which, he said, they were to celebrate.

"We will, however," he added, "not wait for Lady Lawley."

He handed Petrina a glass of champagne and lifted his own as he said:

"To the most magnificent driver and someone so beautiful and so kind that I have no words in which to tell her how much I love her!"

Petrina blushed and turned aside.

"You must not talk to me like that," she said. "You know how angry the Earl would be."

"The Earl is not with us," Lord Rowlock replied, "and at the moment I feel I am the happiest and luckiest man in the world."

"I am so glad I won, for your sake," Petrina said, "but I am afraid Lady Lawley will be very annoyed."

"Furious!" Lord Rowlock agreed, and they both laughed.

He ordered food. Although Petrina felt they ought to wait for their opponents, she had only eaten a small meal before she left London and she was easily persuaded into sampling some slices of cold turkey and a freshly baked cake which had just come from the oven.

"You must rest," Lord Rowlock said when they

had finished. "I expect you will want to drive me home, and driving is quite a strenuous exercise when you are travelling as fast as we have done."

It was true, Petrina thought, and she allowed him to make her comfortable in a big arm-chair and put a stool under her feet.

She leant back against the cushions and realised she did in fact feel a little sleepy.

Perhaps it was the champagne, or perhaps the re-action after the tension of driving, and of course being upset by the Earl being so angry with her.

Whatever the reasons, she awoke with a start to realise that she had fallen asleep.

It was very quiet in the small room and for a moment she could not think where she was.

Then she realised that Lord Rowlock was sitting in the window, looking out into the garden.

"I have been asleep," Petrina said.

"You had every justification for feeling tired," he said caressingly.

He rose as he spoke and came across the room to stand beside her chair and look down at her.

"You look very lovely when you are asleep."

Petrina sat up and put her hands up to her hair.

"You should have awakened me," she said firmly. "What is the time?"

Lord Rowlock pulled out his watch.

"Nearly five o'clock."

Petrina gave a little cry of sheer horror.

"Five o'clock? Then we must go back to London immediately!"

She thought as she spoke that she would not get back until long after the Earl, and there would inevitably be explanations to be made and he would be angry with her for having disobeyed his orders and been with Lord Rowlock.

"We must go," she said firmly. "But what has happened to Lady Lawley?"

Lord Rowlock shrugged his shoulders.

"Perhaps she had an accident. Perhaps she could not find this Inn."

"It seems extraordinary that she has not turned up."

"I agree, but she may have felt that she had lost the race and was too piqued to face us."

"I must get back at once," Petrina said urgently, rising to her feet.

"I will order the curricle."

Lord Rowlock opened the door and Petrina ran upstairs to the bed-room she had used before.

She put on her bonnet and when she looked at her reflection in the mirror she realised her eyes were anxious and worried in a different way from what they had been before.

The Earl was very angry with her already and she had no desire to incense him further.

Now she told herself that it was foolish, perhaps childish, to have come here with Lord Rowlock.

She went down the oak stairs to find him waiting at the bottom of them.

She looked at him and realised from his expression that something serious had occurred, and she asked:

"What is the matter?"

"One of the horses has dropped a shoe."

"Oh, no!" Petrina exclaimed.

"It is all right," he said soothingly. "The blacksmith is only a quarter of a mile away and I have sent a groom to fetch him here at once."

"It means further delay," Petrina said almost frantically.

"There is nothing we can do about it," Lord Rowlock replied.

"No, of course not," she agreed, "but it will make

me even later than I was already. Why, or why did you not wake me?"

"You must not be angry with me," he said. "I knew you were tired, and quite frankly, I was waiting for Lady Lawley to arrive at any moment."

Petrina felt it was a somewhat feeble excuse, but she really had no-one to blame but herself, so she said nothing.

"I will go and see if there is any sign of the blacksmith," Lord Rowlock said and left her alone.

Petrina walked about the small room, feeling frantically that there was something she ought to do, but she was not certain what it was.

It was some time before Lord Rowlock returned.

"Is the blacksmith here?" she asked quickly before he could speak.

He shook his head.

"The ostlers say he will not be long."

"We could hire another horse," Petrina suggested.

"I should think it would be impossible," Lord Rowlock answered, "and even if there was one, it would hardly travel quicker than our own pair."

"No, of course not," Petrina agreed, "at the same time . . ."

"I will go and see if there is anything I can do," Lord Rowlock said before she could say any more.

He was gone for so long that Petrina felt that he must be supervising the shoeing of the horse, but when at last he appeared she knew before he spoke what he had to say.

"The blacksmith is not here?" she asked.

"The groom I sent to find him has returned to say he is away from home. They are expecting him at any moment and he will come straight here the second he walks into his house."

"What can we do?" Petrina asked desperately.

"You will have to be sensible about this, Petrina,"

Lord Rowlock answered. "It is all very unfortunate, but there is nothing we can do about it. What I am going to suggest is that we have something to eat and drink, then the moment the horse is ready we will leave for London, and get there just as quickly as we possibly can."

What he said was so sensible that there was nothing Petrina could do but agree.

Reluctantly she took off her bonnet again, and although she did not feel hungry she realised there was no point in refusing to eat anything, and chose several dishes that the Inn-keeper suggested to her although it was far less than Lord Rowlock ordered.

Because she felt it would make her feel less agitated she accepted a small glass of madeira, and once again Lord Rowlock ordered a bottle of champagne before he went outside to find out what was happening.

When he returned, Petrina thought despairingly that it was getting later and later and when she finally reached London the Earl would undoubtedly be so angry with her that there was every chance of her being sent to Harrogate as a punishment.

When the food came Lord Rowlock made every effort to amuse and entertain her.

She tried to tell herself there was no point in being unpleasant to him for something that was not his fault.

She had agreed only too willingly to come on this mad escapade and she must not blame him for her own stupidity.

Lord Rowlock pressed her to have some champagne but she drank very little of it, feeling it had betrayed her once before in sleeping when she should not have done so.

During dinner he complimented her and made love to her in a way which Petrina felt the Earl would consider extremely reprehensible.

Several times she tried to make him talk on other

subjects, but always he got back to the fact of how much he loved her, how unhappy he had been when she no longer consented to see him.

"I lost my heart the moment I saw you," he said, "and it is ironic that the one person I have ever wanted to marry for herself should have an insurmountable barrier in the shape of her fortune."

"Surely the blacksmith should have arrived?" Petrina interrupted.

She found it difficult to concentrate on what Lord Rowlock was saying because her thoughts kept returning to the Earl and how angry he would be.

"I am sure he has," Lord Rowlock said soothingly.

He went from the room and the maids came in to remove the dishes, leaving only a decanter of port on the table.

"I do not think we need anything more to drink," Petrina said as they set down two glasses on a tray beside it.

"The gentleman ordered the port, Ma'am."

There was nothing Petrina could say to this, but she could not help thinking that Lord Rowlock was not expecting to make an early departure.

The whole thing was extremely unfortunate, first that she had been stupid enough to come so long a way from London that whatever had happened she would have returned much later than she had expected.

Secondly, that the horse should not only have cast a shoe but that the blacksmith was not at home.

"He must be here by now, he must!" Petrina murmured to herself beneath her breath.

As she spoke Lord Rowlock came back.

"He is here?" she asked eagerly.

He shook his head.

"But this is impossible!" Petrina exclaimed. "I insist that we hire a carriage—there must be one available—and travel back to London with one horse."

"I am afraid that is impossible."

"But why?" Petrina asked. "There must be a carriage or a gig of some sort that is available."

"Even if there is," Lord Rowlock said, "I have no intention of asking for it."

She looked at him in surprise, then was very still.

"What are you . . . saying?"

"I am telling you, Petrina, that I love you, and we are not going back to London tonight. We are going to stay here!"

Her eyes widened and looked at him in horror.

He came nearer to her with a smile on his lips.

"I have wanted you and loved you ever since we first met," he said. "Your Guardian drove me out of his house, and I saw later that I had been absurdly weak and spineless in accepting his decision that we should not communicate with each other again."

"What are you saying?" Petrina asked again almost beneath her breath.

"I am telling you that we are going to stay here tonight," Lord Rowlock replied, "and when we return to London tomorrow the Earl will be only too willing to give his consent to our marriage—there will be nothing else he can do."

"Are you crazy?"

"Yes," he replied. "Crazy for you, as I always have been. I love you, Petrina!"

"I am not going to stay here!" she cried. "I am going back to London now, even if I have to walk!"

She ran towards the door as she spoke, but she had only taken two steps in its direction before Lord Rowlock's arms were round her and he held her against him.

"You are staying," he said, "because I want you and there is no escape, little Petrina. So make the best of it!"

"How dare you! How dare you touch me!" Petrina stormed.

Now she was struggling, fighting him with every ounce of strength she had.

She realised he was very strong and she was helpless in his arms.

He folded her close against him, and although she was twisting, struggling, and endeavouring to push him away from her, every effort she made was completely ineffective and he was only laughing at her struggles.

"We will be very happy together," he said. "You are everything I want in a wife and I will teach you to love me as I love you."

"Never! Never! I do not love you, I hate you!"

"Then I shall have to change your mind."

Petrina went on struggling, but she knew she was weakening.

The fact that he had imprisoned her arms made her realise how ineffective her efforts to escape were and that it was only a question of time before she wore herself out against his superior strength.

With an effort she tried to think clearly and change her tactics.

She ceased struggling and looking up at him said:

"Let me go . . . you know there could be no happiness for either of us if I was . . . forced to marry you."

"There would be every happiness for me," Lord Rowlock replied with a smile, and she knew he was thinking of her fortune.

Too late she realised that the whole thing had been a plot from start to finish; that Lord Rowlock had only put this plan into operation when the Duke had told him at Vauxhall Gardens that he was not determined enough.

He must have been waiting for an opportunity to get in touch with her, and she had fallen into the trap he had set for her in such a foolish, idiotic manner that there was no excuse.

"Please listen to me," she said desperately. "If you take me back to London now, I promise that I will help you with money and will not allow the Earl to hurt you or make any trouble for you."

"He will not do that when you are my wife."

"I cannot marry you . . . I have no wish to."

"You will have to marry me," he answered. "And we will find life very amusing when we can afford to do all the things I want to do."

Petrina knew that he felt that her fortune was already within his grasp, and she knew he was right in saying that if they spent the night together in this small Inn there would be nothing she could do but marry him as soon as it could be arranged.

With a sense of horror at what he intended, she knew in that moment that she loved the Earl so overwhelmingly that even to be touched by another man would seem a degradation beyond words.

"Please . . . please," she said frantically, "just listen to me."

"It is too late for words," Lord Rowlock answered. "I find you extremely desirable and I am looking forward to our night of love."

He bent his head as he spoke to find her lips, and she twisted her face from side to side, knowing it was only a matter of time before he would kiss her as he wished to do.

Then as she thought despairingly that there was no hope of escape and that she had lost all hope of happiness, she realised that as they struggled he had moved her backwards against a side-table on which had stood the cold meats that had been offered at dinner.

She put her hand to steady herself against it and her fingers felt something.

Chapter Seven

The Earl, having gone to Osterley Park and had luncheon afterwards with the Earl of Jersey, drove back to London with a feeling of urgency to be home.

He had found it difficult to concentrate even on the mill, which had been a good one, or on the treasures that the Earl had shown him in his superb house, which had been decorated by Adam.

Instead, he kept seeing Petrina's unhappy face and hearing the anguished note in her voice when she had pleaded with him to understand why she had behaved as she had.

When his temper had abated the Earl had realised quite clearly what had motivated her into trying to find a story for the newspaper reporter in order to prevent him from publishing that which concerned himself and Lady Isolda.

He understood now why Lady Isolda had been so insistent on remaining behind after the Prince Regent and the other guests had left.

She had told the Earl that she had something of great importance to impart to him, but he had realised when they were alone that the only thing of importance as far as she was concerned was that he should make love to her.

This was something he had no intention of doing in his own house with his grandmother asleep upstairs.

They had verbally duelled and sparred with each other until only by being determined to the point of rudeness did the Earl persuade her to leave.

He had then made it obvious to Lady Isolda that their liaison was at an end and he realised now why she had not made a scene.

She had in fact been surprisingly unmoved and he now knew it was because she was confident that whatever he said, he would be pressured into marrying her.

As the Earl drove back to London he thought that the real reason why he had lost his temper with Petrina was that he disliked her being aware of the machinations of the two women on whom he had bestowed his favours.

He had always disapproved of Petrina coming into contact with the seamier side of life.

He had in fact been horrified that she should have fixed her interest on the poor prostitutes, even while he knew their cause was one of injustice and suffering.

He knew she was exceptional in that she was not only sensitive but had very deep feelings for those less fortunate than herself.

While he admired her for her desire to help, he considered it his duty as her Guardian to tell her not to.

It was so like Petrina, he thought, to stumble inadvertently on the tangled relationship between himself, Yvonne Vouvray, and the Duke.

When the *Courier* had appeared, carrying the story of the fire in Paradise Row, the Earl had to put up with a great deal of good-natured chaff from his friends and the open sneers of his enemies.

He had been too successful as a sportsman and too outstanding a social figure for people to miss enjoying the feeling that his mistress by being unfaithful to him behind his back had taken him down a peg or two.

The Earl accepted everything that was said to him with a cynical smile and an imperturbable good humour which took much of the satisfaction away from those who baited him.

But secretly, inside himself, he was furious at being humiliated, and he knew now that he had disliked more than anything else the fact that Petrina should be aware of it.

For the first time in his life he questioned his own behaviour and felt something suspiciously like shame.

Ruthlessly he had sent a message to Yvonne Vouvray, telling her to move out of his house in Paradise Row.

But, as he might have anticipated, she had already expected this to happen and had availed herself of the protection of an exceedingly rich, elderly Peer who had been pursuing her for some time.

She had of course not returned the expensive jewellery which the Earl had given her, nor the carriage and horses.

The Earl had made no effort to reproach the Duke or alter in any way his usual acknowledgement of their acquaintance.

He knew the young nobleman was nervous, he knew there was speculation in the Clubs as to whether he would "call him out," but it was characteristic of the Earl that having made a bad bargain he was prepared to forget it.

But Petrina's revelation of her part in the episode had made this impossible. And the Earl found himself not only angry at the way he had been treated, but exceedingly annoyed that it should have involved anyone so young and so lovely as his Ward.

By the time the Earl reached London he was regretting the things he had said to Petrina and determined to make amends.

He now understood that she had done what she thought was best for him.

It was reprehensible of course that a débutante should be involved in such matters, but Petrina was not the ordinary type of débutante who would either have been deeply shocked at what she heard or else giggled about it with her friends.

"She has courage," the Earl told himself, "and the most imaginative mind I have ever encountered."

Only Petrina, he thought with a somewhat rueful smile, could have concocted anything so fantastic as driving Yvonne Vouvray and the Duke into the street inadequately clothed because fireworks had been lit in the basement area of the house.

The more he thought about it the more he found it amusing, and by the time he was tooling his horses through the traffic-laden streets he could genuinely laugh about the whole affair.

He almost wished he had seen the Duke wearing nothing but a bed-spread over a pair of pantaloons and Yvonne in a diaphanous negligé surrounded by Firemen.

He had been shown the cartoon that had been drawn of the incident and he told himself that he would undoubtedly keep a copy to remind himself in future to put no trust in "Lady-Birds," as Petrina had called them.

He was still smiling when he drove his horses up Park Lane and into the drive of Staverton House.

It was six-thirty P.M. and he decided that he would not dine at White's with his friends as he had promised, but instead would stay at home and make amends to Petrina for his bad temper.

The Major Domo, however, informed him that Miss Lyndon had not returned.

"She went driving, M'Lord, at about one o'clock."

"With whom?" the Earl enquired.

"I regret, M'Lord, that as I was belowstairs she was seen off by one of the footmen, who did not know the name of the gentleman who called for her, although he says he has seen him here in the past."

The Earl wondered who it could be and went upstairs to his grandmother's room.

She looked up with delight at seeing him.

"Did you enjoy yourself at Osterley Park?" she enquired.

"It is certainly a magnificent house," the Earl answered. "Who is Petrina with?"

"Petrina?" the Dowager Duchess asked. "I have not seen her since this morning. I am afraid that I have been sleeping the whole afternoon."

"I expect she will be back shortly," the Earl said, anxious not to upset his grandmother.

He knew that she, like most elderly people, was given to worrying over small things.

He went to his own room to change, but learnt when he went downstairs before dinner that Petrina had still not returned.

He waited for over an hour, then in an ill humour sat down to dinner alone.

He thought it extremely remiss on Petrina's part if she intended to dine with friends not to have sent a message to inform his grandmother that she was not returning until later.

It was unlike her, because ever since she had come to Staverton House she had always shown the Dowager Duchess the most exquisite courtesy and good manners, which had delighted the older woman.

The Earl had the uncomfortable feeling that perhaps, because Petrina was so upset by what he had said to her, she was deliberately delaying her return in case he should continue to berate her.

He could not help remembering that he had told her to get out of his sight and he wished that he had chosen his words more carefully or rather had tried from the beginning to understand the motive behind her behaviour.

When dinner was over the Earl repaired to his Library with instructions that he was to be notified the moment Petrina returned.

He read the day's newspapers and picked up a book which so far he had found absorbing, but he was unable to concentrate on it.

He found himself continually looking at the clock and despite every resolution to the contrary he found his anger rising again.

"It is ridiculous of Petrina to disappear like this," he said to himself.

Just as he was about to ring the bell to ask if by any chance she had returned without his knowledge, the door opened and Petrina came in.

He had been about to reproach her for causing him anxiety, then he took one glance at her and the words died on his lips.

He had only to look at her pale face, the stricken expression in her eyes, and her hair, which had been blown untidily about her uncovered head, to know that something very untoward had occurred.

Petrina stood looking at him and he saw that she was trembling.

"What has happened?" he asked.

For a moment it seemed as if she could not reply. Then in a hoarse little voice, speaking so low that he could hardly hear the words, she answered:

"I . . . I have . . . killed a m-man . . . and stolen a chaise!"

She swayed as she spoke and in two steps the Earl was at her side.

Her body sagged against his as he put his arms round her and drew her to the sofa.

"Forgive me . . . forgive me!" she murmured unhappily.

The Earl laid her back against the cushions and went to the grog-tray to pour out a little brandy.

He carried it to her side, sat down, put his arm round her, and lifted the glass to her lips.

"Drink!" he said. "Then you can tell me what has happened."

She took a sip, then shook her head, hating the taste of it.

"Drink more!" the Earl said firmly.

Because she was too weak to argue she did as he told her.

She felt the fiery spirit course down her throat to take away the darkness that had seemed to rise up from the floor to encompass her.

When she raised her hand to push aside the half-empty glass, the Earl set it down on the table beside the sofa. Then he said quietly and calmly in his deep voice:

"Now tell me what has occurred."

Petrina's eyes were dark and frightened as she raised them to his.

"I . . . I killed him," she said. "I . . . killed him."

"Killed whom?"

"Lord . . . Rowlock!"

The Earl's lips tightened, but still quietly he said, in a voice without expression:

"Suppose you tell me exactly what happened."

Hesitatingly, stumbling over her words but somehow able to speak because she was holding on tightly to the Earl's hand, Petrina explained how she had met Lord Rowlock in the Park, and that because she was so hurt and unhappy at what the Earl had said to her she had accepted his invitation to race Lady Lawley.

"I think now," she said miserably, "that I was . . . not racing . . . anyone. It was . . . just an excuse on the part of Lord Rowlock to . . . get me . . . to go away with him."

The Earl encouraged her to continue and she told him how she had fallen asleep at the Plume of Feathers, and then that Lord Rowlock had discovered that one of the horses had cast a shoe.

She looked up at the Earl as she spoke and saw a cynical twist to his lips as he said:

"It is a trick as old as hell, but you were not to know that."

She told him how they had had dinner while they were supposedly waiting for the blacksmith to arrive, and how when the meal was ended Lord Rowlock had admitted to her that he had planned all along for her to stay the night with him, so that she would be forced to marry him.

"I knew then," Petrina said in a broken little voice, "how ... foolish I had been to ... go with him in the ... first place. I tried to ... run away ... b-but he was strong and I knew I was ... helpless once he put his ... arms round me."

Her voice died away on a little sob and after a moment the Earl asked:

"What happened?"

"As I was ... struggling he had b-backed me against a side-table," Petrina answered. "There had been c-cold dishes on it when we were having dinner. I put out my hand ... I felt the handle of a ... knife."

Her fingers tightened convulsively on the Earl's.

"I ... knew it was the only ... thing that could s-save me," she faltered.

The Earl did not speak and after a moment she went on:

"His arms held m-mine to my sides ... and I could only just m-move my hand ... but I ..."

Again her voice died away and the Earl asked:

"What did you do?"

"I d-drove the ... knife with all my f-force into his ... stomach!"

She gave a little cry.

"It was horrible! It went in so easily . . . right up to the hilt . . . and for a moment he did not m-move . . . then he screamed and fell d-down."

The Earl felt Petrina shivering as if with the shock.

"He lay there and the blood began to . . . ooze out . . . crimson . . . all over him."

"What did you do?" the Earl asked.

"I could not look . . . I could not s-stand there . . . and I was sure he was . . . dead!"

She drew in her breath as if remembering how terrifying it had been.

"I ran out of the room . . . down the passage . . . the door of the Inn was . . . open and outside I saw a . . . c-curricle. It was not a smart one like yours . . . but it was drawn by two horses . . . and there was a g-groom holding the reins."

There was a little pause before she forced herself to continue:

"I r-ran to the side of the curricle and s-said:

" 'There has been an accident! Your master needs you immediately! I will hold the horses for you.' "

"He believed you?" the Earl asked.

"He handed me the reins," Petrina replied, "and I climbed into the driver's seat and drove off."

The Earl could not help thinking she had been rather ingenious in effecting her escape.

"I thought I heard someone shouting after me," Petrina said, "but I did not look back. I whipped up the horses . . . drove onto the main road and . . . set off for London."

She told the Earl how she had soon discovered that she was not as far from London as she had thought and that Lord Rowlock must have taken her by a far longer route than was necessary in order to prolong the time it took them to reach the Plume of Feathers.

Then as her narrative came to an end Petrina's

head dropped low and she said in a small, frightened voice:

"He is . . . dead . . . I am sure of it."

"That is something I will find out," the Earl said.

She looked up at him questioningly and he went on:

"I will not only discover whether Lord Rowlock is dead, but I will also return the chaise you—borrowed. I have no wish for you to be branded as a thief."

He was smiling as he spoke but as he would have risen to his feet Petrina held on tightly to his hand with both of hers.

"Do not . . . leave me!" she begged.

"I have to for a little while," the Earl replied, "but I will not be longer than I can help. Stay here, or go to bed, Petrina. I will come and tell you exactly what has happened as soon as I return."

He rose, but she still would not let him go.

"I am . . . sorry," she said. "Terribly . . . terribly sorry that I should have caused a . . . scandal, which I know you will . . . hate."

"There will be no scandal if I can help it," the Earl said firmly. "Do not despair, Petrina. Things may not be as bad as you think."

He took his hand from hers, then he bent down to put his arm under her legs to turn her round so that she was lying on the sofa.

"Go to sleep," he said. "You are tired out and it is not surprising. Nothing is more exhausting than fear."

She looked up at him, her eyes very large in her pale face.

"I will be as quick as I can," the Earl promised, and bending kissed her lips.

It was only a light kiss that he might have given to a child.

But he knew as he went from the room that it was not a child he had kissed, nor was there anything childish in the response he felt.

Petrina lay on the sofa where he had left her and told herself that the most wonderful thing she had ever known in her whole life was the touch of his lips on hers.

She knew he had only kissed her to reassure and comfort her after all she had been through, but because she loved him everything else she was feeling was swept aside by the leap of her heart and a rapture such as she had not known it was possible to feel.

He had kissed her!

That was something she would be able to remember for the rest of her life, then insidiously the thought came to her that perhaps she would not have a very long life.

After all, she had killed a man, and the penalty for murder was death.

Petrina had read of the horrors of condemned criminal suffered in Newgate Prison before he was hanged or alternatively—which was considered a more merciful sentence—transported.

Everything she had read about the sufferings of those condemned to prison or sent to Australia seemed to rise up and haunt her and with a little cry she put her hands over her face.

Then she began to wonder if in fact the Earl would reach the Plume of Feathers to find out what had happened before the Police came to Staverton House in search of her.

Supposing, she asked herself, the Landlord finding the dead man had immediately alerted the Constabulary and she was arrested before the Earl returned to support her?

She did not know whether or not the Inn-keeper was aware of her identity.

Lord Rowlock may have told him who she was and even, as Nicholas Thornton had done, given her name as a guarantee that the bill would be paid.

Because everything she thought of frightened her,

Petrina rose to her feet, and as she could not lie down or rest as the Earl had told her to do, she went upstairs to her own room.

She did not ring for her maid but looked at herself in the mirror and was appalled at what she saw.

When she had left the Plume of Feathers she had no bonnet on her head and her hair was in wild disarray.

Her gown, too, from her struggle with Lord Rowlock and because she had worn it all day was creased besides being dusty.

She pulled it off and flung it on the ground, then having washed went to the wardrobe.

As she opened the doors she could not help wondering what was the best gown to wear in prison and found herself shivering again with sheer terror.

She found herself listening in case she should hear voices coming up the stairs and waited for a knock on the door of a servant to tell her that the Police were waiting below.

"I must hide!" Petrina told herself. "I must hide somewhere safe until the Earl returns."

Hastily she put on another gown and taking down a dark velvet cloak put it over her shoulders.

Her reticule containing money was in a drawer of her dressing-table.

A few minutes later she opened the door of her bed-room, and so as not to be seen by the footmen on duty in the Hall, she went down another staircase.

This led her to the passage in which was situated Mr. Richardson's office.

She went to the door and listened, but there was no sound and she was quite certain that by now he would have retired to his own apartments in another part of the house.

She opened the door cautiously.

There was one oil-lamp burning, but it was enough for her to see clearly what she sought.

Moving almost like a shadow, she went to the board on the wall and without difficulty, because the keys were all labelled, found the two which belonged to the house in Paradise Row.

She took one, then letting herself out onto the terrace she ran across the garden to the gate in the wall.

*   *   *

Petrina opened the front door of the house in Paradise Row.

It was in darkness, but because she remembered the plan that Nicholas Thornton had shown her she felt her way with outstretched hands through the small Hall and into a room on the right of it.

This she was sure was a large Salon running the full length of the house, with windows looking both onto the street and onto the garden at the back.

She had expected the room to be empty, but she stumbled against a chair, and realised that her feet were moving on a carpet.

Slowly, frightened that she might fall, she found her way to a sofa and sat down on it.

She had before leaving Staverton House scribbled a note to the Earl, which she had left on her pillow.

She knew that if he did not find her in the Library he would go upstairs, as he had promised, to her bedroom.

She told him where she had gone, knowing that if she did not find the keys as she expected in the Secretary's room, she would have to go upstairs again, for there was nowhere else in London where she could hide.

Now she only had to wait, and she found herself planning that if the Earl thought she was in danger of being arrested he could give her the money to go abroad or to Scotland where no-one would be able to find her.

It was frightening to think she might have to live
alone and perhaps in disguise for the rest of her life ...
so frightening that Petrina wondered if it would not be
better to die and get it over.

She was quite certain that because of what she had
done there could be no happiness for her in the future
and the Earl would never forgive her for causing a
scandal.

Anyway, he was so angry with her that though he
had been kind in listening to her story, that was not
to say that she did not still disgust him as he had told
her she did when he learnt about the fireworks.

"I love him! I love him!" Petrina whispered to herself, and felt again the pressure of his lips on hers
and the sensations of joy the kiss had aroused in her
breast.

'He is so magnificent ... so wonderful in every
way,' she thought. 'How could I expect for one moment that he would even think of me except as a tiresome child?'

He certainly had had no wish to be her Guardian
and she remembered how reluctant he had been to
accept the responsibility.

How could she ever have imagined, she thought,
that she would fall in love with him and that even to
be in the same house with him was a joy and a delight
beyond all dreams?

"At least he has kissed me," she told herself, and
wondered unhappily what lay ahead of her in the future.

She wondered too if he agreed that she should
go away into hiding, whether, if she asked him to do
so, he would kiss her again.

She wanted to feel his arms round her, she wanted
him to take possession of her lips as Lord Rowlock
had tried to do.

Then she told herself she was being presumptuous

or, as the Earl would say, impertinent in even imagining such a thing.

Time seemed to pass very slowly, so slowly that Petrina, sitting tense and rigid in the darkness, began to think that perhaps the Earl, when he found she had left Staverton House, had decided to abandon her.

He would not care that she was in an empty house alone. Perhaps he would think it was the best way to be rid of her and forget her very existence.

And perhaps, she thought suddenly, he would be even more disgusted with her than he was already because she had come to the house where he had kept his mistress.

For the first time since leaving Staverton House Petrina began to question her own wisdom in running away.

Now she thought she could smell on the air the fragrance of the perfume used by Yvonne Vouvray, and she imagined she could hear the Earl's voice speaking to her of love and her soft exquisite tones with a broken accent answering him.

Petrina gave a little cry and put her hands over her ears as if to blot out her own imaginings.

Then as she took them away she was aware that she was not alone.

Someone had come into the house without her hearing them—or perhaps they had been there all the time.

There was someone standing just inside the door of the room and as she held her breath she heard her name.

"Petrina!"

There was no mistaking the deep voice which had spoken, and with a cry that seemed to echo in the darkness Petrina rose to her feet and ran to where she knew he was standing.

The Earl put his arms round her and felt her body soft, warm, and frantic against his.

He held her very close.

"It is all right," he said soothingly. "He is not dead."

Petrina's face had been hidden against his shoulder and now she raised it.

"He is . . . not dead?"

She could hardly say the words and they were little louder than a sigh.

"He is alive, though you were very rough with him," the Earl answered. "But he thoroughly deserved it!"

Petrina hid her face once more against his shoulder, conscious of an inexpressible relief which was mixed with the wonder of feeling the Earl's arms holding her so tightly.

"Are you . . . sure?" she asked a little incoherently.

"Quite sure!" the Earl replied; and there was a hint of amusement in his voice as he added, "So it is quite unnecessary for you to hide from the Police and you can come home, my darling!"

Petrina was suddenly very still.

As she raised her face, thinking she could not have heard him aright, the Earl's lips came down on hers.

For one moment she thought she was dreaming, then the wonder that he had evoked in her before was intensified until she felt as if in the darkness she no longer existed but became a part of him.

It was as if he took her heart and soul into his keeping and she gave him not only her love but her self until she was his completely, as she had longed to be.

His lips became more demanding, more possessive, and she felt as if they were enveloped by a light which was part of all beauty and of life itself.

"I love you!" she wanted to say, but there were no words to express what she felt and she thought that they were no longer human beings but gods.

He carried her away from the world and up into the sky and she was part of the moon and the stars, while a light from the sun enveloped them.

It was a kiss so perfect, so wonderful, that Petrina felt she must have died and was in Heaven.

Finally, after a long time, the Earl raised his head.

"My precious!" he said, and his voice was deep and a little unsteady. "There is no-one so unpredictable and incorrigible and yet I would not have you otherwise."

"I love you!" Petrina whispered, hardly aware of what she was saying or doing. Bemused, bewildered, she felt enchanted by his lips.

"I love you, too!"

Although she could not see him she stared up in the darkness.

"You . . . love me?" she whispered. "Is that . . . really true?"

"Really true!" the Earl replied. "But, my darling one, this is hardly the place in which I should be telling you so."

"Does it matter where it is?" Petrina asked. "I have longed and prayed for you to have a little . . . affection for me . . . but I never thought you would . . . love me."

"I fought against it," the Earl admitted, "as I fought against loving anyone, but I cannot help my feelings about you, Petrina. I knew when I was ready to save you from the consequences of any crime you had committed that I could not live without you!"

Petrina gave a little cry that was one of sheer happiness.

The Earl's arms tightened round her.

"If you had killed Rowlock we would have gone abroad together."

"You really . . . mean that you would have . . . come with me?" Petrina asked.

"Do you think I could have let you go alone?" the Earl asked almost harshly.

Then he laughed.

"God knows, you get into enough trouble when I am there, so I cannot begin to imagine what would happen to you if I was not."

"All I want is to . . . be with . . . you," Petrina said. "Always and for . . . ever!"

"And that is exactly what you will be," the Earl replied, "although I tremble to think what sort of life you will lead me into."

"I will be good . . . I will do . . . anything you ask of me," Petrina said with a passionate note in her voice.

She paused, then she asked, as if she was afraid:

"You do . . . mean it? You really mean it when you . . . say you . . . love me?"

"I mean it!" the Earl answered. "And I will make you believe it, my sweet, however long it takes me to convince you."

Petrina drew in her breath.

"Please . . ." she whispered, "please . . . kiss me . . . again."

The Earl's lips were on hers and once again she felt as if he lifted her into the sky.

His kiss became more passionate, more demanding, and she felt a sudden flicker of a flame within her body which seemed to join with the ecstasy of her mind and make the sensations she felt more intense and more wonderful than they had been before.

She could feel his heart beating against hers and knew that she excited him.

"I love you! I love you!" she murmured as he set her free.

"And I love you, my adorable, unpredictable darling!" he answered. "Come—let us go home."

He put his arm round her to draw her towards the door, and with their other hands outstretched to prevent themselves from knocking against the furniture, they found their way linked together to the door.

"This place is an aptly named Paradise," Petrina

whispered as she felt the night air cold against her face.

The Earl bent to kiss her forehead, then they walked out to where she saw his closed carriage was waiting.

He handed her into it, then as a footman shut the door he pulled her once again into his arms.

She put her head against his shoulder with a little sigh of utter happiness and asked:

"Tell me what happened?"

"I rode to the Plume of Feathers," the Earl answered. "One of my grooms came with me, leading a spare horse, the other drove back the chaise you had purloined in such a high-handed manner."

"Was the owner very . . . angry?"

"When I arrived at the Inn," the Earl went on, "and incidentally it took me only three quarters of an hour to get there, I walked in to find half a dozen men in the Taproom talking loudly. They looked round at my entrance and I asked:

" 'Has anyone here lost a chaise and two horses?'

"For a moment there was a stupefied silence, then an elderly gentleman, a typical country Squire, answered:

" 'My chaise has been stolen, Sir!'

" 'Then I have the pleasure of returning it to you,' I told him. 'I found it on the roadside, unattended, the horses cropping the grass on the verge.' "

The Earl smiled.

"There was a great deal of excitement about this, and when I could make myself heard I asked:

" 'What had happened? Why did you think it was stolen?'

" 'It was taken by a Droxy from London, Sir,' the Inn-keeper explained, 'she came here with a nobleman called Lord Rowlock.'

" 'What happened?' I asked.

" 'Really wicked, she were,' the Inn-keeper replied.

'She quarrels with the gentleman, then stabs him in the belly wi' a knife!'

" 'Good heavens!' I exclaimed. 'Is he badly injured?'

" 'Bad enough' the Inn-keeper answered. 'The Surgeon says he must be carefully nursed for several weeks before he can rise from his bed.'

" 'How very inconvenient for you!' I commiserated.

"The Inn-keeper winked at me.

" 'We be short o' guests at the moment, Sir.'

" 'Then I feel sure you will look after him very well,' I said."

Petrina gave a deep sigh.

"I thought he must be . . . dead because he . . . bled so much."

"Forget it," the Earl said sharply. "You are not to think of him again."

"Do you . . . forgive me for . . . accepting his . . . invitation?"

"I will forgive you if you promise me that you will never drive anyone's horses except mine."

Petrina gave her little chuckle.

"As if I would want to! No-one has such superb horses as you."

"I shall be jealous of my horses if they prevent you from thinking of me."

"You know I have no wish to think of anything or anybody except . . . you," Petrina answered. "I still cannot believe that you really . . . love me, not after I have behaved so . . . badly."

She saw by the light of gas-lamps they were passing that the Earl was smiling.

"I can see that you are in urgent need of someone to keep you in order, and as your husband I will be more fitted for the post than anyone else."

"Will you . . . really marry me?" Petrina whispered.

"You are not, I hope, suggesting that you should occupy any other position in my life?" the Earl questioned.

She blushed, knowing how much he disapproved of her interest in "Lady-birds."

"Supposing I . . . disappoint you?" she said quickly. "Or get into trouble so that you grow to . . . hate me?"

"You will not disappoint me," the Earl said firmly. "You may make me anxious, apprehensive, and even angry at times, but I shall still love you, darling. Because I have never known anyone quite like you and I have never before been so enchanted!"

"You say such wonderful, perfect things to me!" Petrina cried. "How can I tell you how much I love you?"

"Just give me your love," the Earl answered. "It is something I want and need, my precious, naughty little Ward."

She clung to him, moving her body a little nearer to his.

"I did not . . . know it was possible to be so . . . happy."

"Neither did I."

He would have kissed her but he realised that the horses had just turned in at the drive of Staverton House.

As Petrina walked into the Hall she felt as if the lights dazzled her and knew it was not just because she was coming in out of the darkness where she had been for so long, but because she was so happy that everything about her had a radiant, fairy-like quality.

They went into the Library and as the door shut behind them she turned to look at the Earl.

She thought it was impossible for any man to look so magnificent, so handsome, and at the same time so authoritative.

She gazed at him. His eyes were on her face and his lips were smiling.

"What are you thinking?" he asked.

"That I am dreaming," Petrina answered, with a

throb in her voice. "That it cannot be . . . true that you love me."

The Earl opened his arms.

"Come here! I will tell you how much."

She ran to him and he pulled her crushingly against him, but when she lifted her face eagerly towards his he looked down at her to say very tenderly:

"I do not believe anyone could be so lovely and at the same time so intriguing and so original."

Petrina drew in her breath and he went on:

"There is something about you, my little love, that is quite irresistible. I find myself thinking about you, remembering what you say, recalling the expression in your eyes and the glint of red in your hair."

He gave a laugh.

"I think you have bewitched me! I never thought it possible for me to feel for any woman as I feel about you."

"Perhaps . . . when you know me better I will . . . bore you," Petrina whispered.

"I think that very unlikely," the Earl replied, "for the simple reason that your mind is as captivating as your face, my darling one. I have never before met a woman who thinks as you do, or, as it happens, feels as you feel."

"What I feel has often made you . . . angry."

"As it will, I am sure, very often in the future," the Earl answered, "but let me tell you it is quite impossible to be bored and angry at the same time."

Petrina laughed.

"It is so exciting! So thrilling to think I can be with you, that I can talk to you and you can teach me."

She thought he looked at her in surprise and she said:

"There are so many things I have wanted you to teach me ever since I have been here, but I did not like to ask so many questions."

She pressed herself closer to him as she said:

"You are so clever, so wise. Will you teach me the things I want to know?"

"I am making no promises," the Earl said warily, "but there is one thing I will teach you, my precious one, which to me is the most important subject of all."

"What is that?" Petrina asked.

"Love," he answered, "and even if you are the most able pupil, I promise you it is going to take a very long time!"

"That is something I . . . want to learn," Petrina whispered.

"There is a lot for me to learn, too," the Earl said. "I know now I have never been in love before I met you."

"Am I . . . different?"

Petrina could not help thinking of the beauty of Lady Isolda and the allure of Yvonne Vouvray.

"Very different," the Earl said firmly, "and this is true, my lovely one, you are the only woman I have ever asked to be my wife."

"I am glad . . . so very . . . very . . . glad."

Now as if she could not wait for his lips she put her arm round his neck and pulled his face down to hers.

"I love you with all of me," she said. "My heart . . . my mind, and . . . my soul are all . . . yours!"

The Earl held her so closely that she could hardly breathe.

His lips came down on hers, holding her completely captive and making the little flame that she felt within her burst into a conflagration that seemed to sear its way burningly through her whole body.

'It is like the fireworks in Paradise Row,' she thought irrepressibly.

Then there was only the moon, the stars, and the light of the sun as the Earl carried her above the world into a Heaven that was all their own.

BARBARA CARTLAND, the celebrated romantic novelist, historian, playwright, lecturer, political speaker, and television personality, has now written over two hundred books. She has had a number of historical books published and several biographical ones, including a biography of her brother, Major Ronald Cartland, who was the first Member of Parliament to be killed in the war. The book has a preface by Sir Winston Churchill.

In private life Barbara Cartland is a Dame of Grace of St. John of Jerusalem and one of the first women, after a thousand years, to be admitted to the Chapter General.

She has fought for better conditions and salaries for midwives and nurses, and, as President of the Hertfordshire Branch of the Royal College of Midwives, she has been invested with the first Badge of Office ever given in Great Britain, which was subscribed to by the midwives themselves.

Barbara Cartland has also championed the cause of old people and founded the first Romany Gypsy Camp in the world. It was christened "Barbaraville" by the gypsies.

Barbara Cartland is deeply interested in Vitamin Therapy and is President of the National Association for Health.

F   3-4-78

Cartland
   Love, lords, and lady-birds